GRANNY

SLEUTHS

By the author

Fiction
Those Among Us
Those Among Us Return

Young Adult Fiction
Grandad's Extraordinary Camper Van
Grandad's Unforgettable Camper Van

The Scott Series
Ten Quests (Book one)
Ten Kingdoms (Book two)
Ten Keys (Book three)
Ten Trolls (Book four)
Ten Discs (Book five)

Anthology
This Way and That
Here, There, and Everywhere

Colouring Books
A Colouring Book for OAPs

GRANNY SLEUTHS

by John Edward Parsons

2024

Cataloguing information
ISBN: 979-8-87256-834-6

Cover design: Global Wordsmiths
Production design: Global Wordsmiths

Acknowledgements

To my wordsmith Nicci, who not just works on my book, but is forever coaxing me to become an even better storyteller.

To Sheila and Gill, who we met on a cruise and became good friends. When we were first talking, they said something which caused the spark for my imagination to start thinking about this story. My two main characters are loosely based on my two friends (I use their first names with their permission), but they are not meant to represent them in any way.

It has been mooted that another story should follow this one with the two ladies once again caught up in a different problem.

It's given me food for thought, but...

Dedication

To my loving wife, Jennifer, who has helped me pull this story together to its end. What would I do without you by my side?

To my sister, who is in hospital with terminal cancer. You are forever in our thoughts.

CHAPTER ONE

November

Robert Price glanced around as potential bargain hunters walking around the warehouse looked at the items that were on sale today. This was a temporarily rented place, as had others been before today. He never held a black auction in the same place, and it was always booked in an alias name so nothing could be traced back to him.

He couldn't help but rub his hands together. Some of the possible purchasers had their assistants following them around, taking note of anything their masters had shown an interest in. One of particular interest to him was the lone Arab. He knew who he represented, and he'd been before. Something had stimulated the interest of an Arab sultan, as it had in the past.

He tapped his slightly protruding belly that pushed over the belt of his trousers; his six-pack had long ago reformed into a beer barrel. Anyone looking at Robert might wonder where he'd come from. In a suit and tie, he looked like a typical businessman, but today, he was an auctioneer. Just short of six feet, he was what one might call slightly rotund. He dressed well and spoke with a certain authority.

Robert wasn't someone you'd call handsome. He was more the rugged hard type. He tanned easily—maybe he had Italian blood mixed in him—and he never burned in the sun. His hair was almost black, curling as it came around the back of his head and, much to his chagrin, highlighting his growing bald spot at the crown. He had boxed in his local club and represented his school, where he received a blow to his nose that left it slightly askew. His opponent didn't win the match; Robert floored him two minutes later.

His schooling had been through a grammar school, where he'd showed an active brain, with mathematics and English literature coming easily to him. As a result of this, he received a grant to attend university. If his CV were readily available, it might show that he was a dropout from university for "lack of endeavour." The fact that he had been found in bed with the administrator's wife, who was quite vocal with her enthusiasm, made it obvious he must leave. But lack of endeavour? That was a grievous claim. He would have finished his endeavour rather happily if the administrator hadn't returned early.

Robert wasn't on any police database, and he was rather pleased with the respectable image he'd cultivated. There had been a few near misses, but he still had a clean sheet. Not that his mug wouldn't enhance the collection of faces the cops had.

With no qualifications, he'd quickly decided he needed to go into business on his own. First, he needed money, and the quickest way was to use someone else's. So started his qualification at the University of Life, and with money in his pocket, he felt he was now competent.

His parents had been mortified that their aspiring boy had left grammar school full of hope for a glorious future but had failed because he was unsuccessful in applying himself to the learning. To them, Robert was a failure. Better they didn't know what he thought his qualifications were now.

Robert had once taken a job in a warehouse packaging company as a processer who checked the labels to the orders. He was called up to the office one day to sack him for theft. They'd discovered that some parcels had new delivery labels put on over the originals. They'd gone to one of those addresses and found it was an empty rental property. They hadn't been able to definitively prove it was Robert, but they showed him a grainy video of him adjusting a label, so he left, still professing his innocence.

His working life had been a succession of near misses. His "stolen to order" car business was hurriedly closed after a raid by the police on the old woollen mill used as the business headquarters the stolen cars were delivered to. The police found seven vehicles, one of which was already loaded onto a container bound for Argentina. Robert's name wasn't on any paperwork seized by the police, so when charges had been made, those caught accepted their fate, and

Robert walked away with a new idea forming in his mind.

He'd noticed that the working class had begun to acquire a taste for wine, so he began to import it from France. Robert organised two cars, driven by paid drivers, to cross over to France, pick up as much wine and spirits as they could, and return through customs, saying it was for a party and thus for their own use.

This worked very well for some time. He employed different drivers with different cars for one-off ventures and paid them well. His lock-up under the railway arches in London was soon stacked with wine, brandy, and cognac. He built a good client base, and profits soon came rolling in.

Robert thought he'd covered all his angles, but one of his drivers got greedy and went back with the same car the next day, trying to return saying the same thing. He was pulled over, the booze confiscated, and he ended up in court.

Even though one of Robert's regular workers told the driver that it was his own fault, and that he should take the punishment and say nothing, Robert was left with no chance of continuing. As the stock diminished, the business ended.

He'd married at an early age and was divorced two years later: another failure. Two extramarital affairs had been the reason. Since then, he'd had no shortage of offers, and women passed in and out of his life. He then started a limousine business and a house removal business, both of which became successful.

People were always moving somewhere, and when he heard of a small, established company about to close down, Robert made the owner an offer he couldn't refuse. He purchased a larger van and employed Barry (Badger) Brooks and his son, John. Business built up. John helped set up the IT side, and Robert acquired a new van as the business grew.

Ever watchful to changes, Robert then purchased his first high-end limo: an almost-new, white Mercedes. Private bookings for chauffeur-driven cars for the rich, and the maybe rich, started to roll in. Now with three cars, this enterprise was very busy.

But today's business in this warehouse was different. He had a partner who had set up this sweet deal. At first, it had been slow, but once they had an item that two or more wanted, the news spread. Now, the bidding paddles held by his collective clients numbered almost twenty.

Robert heard the rain outside that must have been coming down in torrents and was glad that the warehouse was just above freezing, though the heating was barely able to make a dent into the pervading chill of the vast building. Priceright (Robert's nickname) watched as one after another, the potential buyers moved around the warehouse examining the items.

Two figurines had caused quite a lot of interest. At just over eighteen inches high, the porcelain figures of Romeo and Juliet were Italian-made and were from a one-off production of just one hundred. They weren't boxed, but not a mark spoiled the pair.

The minimum value of these figures had been set at £16,000. One of the top auction houses had sold a set just over a year ago; the starting price had been £18,000, and the sale ended at £27,500. A pretty price and a tidy profit indeed.

All of the buyers were aware that this was a sale of stolen wares of only the best quality. Some items were destined to go to a collector, bought through their agents and never to be seen by the ex-owner again. Others would be exported and sold to private buyers.

Everything had been photographed, described, and listed when something of its like had been last sold and the value it had made. The file had been uploaded to the cloud with a code number to it. Those who had shown an interest had been mailed the code number, and they downloaded it to look at the latest stock.

Business had been very good over the past few years, and the number of punters was growing.

Requests for certain items of interest had been left in the messenger on the dark web, and once the sale was over, the site would be closed, routes and trails killed, and John would set up another site.

Badger, who had become Robert's right-hand man in this venture, nudged him and pointed to his watch.

Robert nodded, moved up onto the staging and rang a bell.

"Okay, ladies and gentlemen. You know how this works. We offer each item below the market price, and you just bid until I end up with one bid. If you place a bid, then you must honour it." He looked around. "Now to item number one, listed at £3,000. Any offers, please?"

Paddles rose and fell with the buyers' interest until the item was at its highest bid. The letter on the paddle was noted, and red stickers were stuck on the item with that letter on it. The letter denoted who the person was who had purchased the item, though no real names were ever exchanged.

Things moved briskly on until the figurines came around. Robert had noted that the Arab flunky had yet to use his paddle. He knew that this would be a good one, which was why he'd left it until the last item to be sold. "Our final item is the rather excellent Italian porcelain figurines of Romeo and Juliet. A limited edition, not likely to come to market again, and perfect, with no marks or chips on either of them. We're starting the bidding at the incredibly low price of £16,000."

The Arab man towards the back held up a paddle with S on it. "My principal offers £20,000."

People around the floor murmured, clearly surprised at the immediate jump in price.

Robert smiled. "We have £20,000 for this rather unique se. Is anyone else interested?"

Paddle C appeared, its wielder offering £21,000. Before Robert could say anything, other paddles rose and fell in quick succession, and they were soon at £31,000.

"The highest offer is £31,000—are you all finished?" Robert pointed to the man with paddle H.

The Arab man once again held up his paddle. "My principal offers £35,000."

Robert grinned inwardly at the thought of all that profit. "We now have an offer of £35,000 for this unique limited-edition pair of figurines. Are there any more bids?"

The owner of the paddle H turned and glared at the Arab. "£36,000."

The Arab chap didn't seem ᵖperturbed. "My principal offers £40,000."

The owner of paddle H shook his head.

Robert's heart pounded with joy. £40,000! If only they could get a hit like that from every job. "I have £40,000 for the Italian figurines. Are there any more bids?" He looked at the owner of the paddle H but received no response. "Going once... Going twice... Sold to the owner of the paddle S for £40,000. Thank you, everyone. If you can have your money ready for your purchases and move to the sale area, we'll be with you shortly."

He stepped down from the stage and watched as his tally clerk busied himself with the calculations. Moments later, he handed Robert a piece of paper. Just over £400,000. Not bad at all.

The Arab gentleman approached Robert. "My principal is very grateful to you. For a small fee, would you be able to arrange for the items to be available with customs clearance for my principal's private plane coming from Oman into Stanstead?"

"How small?" Always it was money with Priceright. As he often said to his clients: we can do anything if the price is right.

***

Twenty-four hours later, Robert looked around the warehouse and nodded to himself.

The Romeo and Juliet figurines had been packed with bubble wrap, straw, and airbags inside a rather large packing crate. Nestled in this cocoon of protective covering, they were ready loaded onto the Arab's private plane when it arrived.

Robert had a network of people he paid for the paperwork and export licence to clear customs and excise. It was an inconvenient expense, but nevertheless, he stuck the labels onto the crate and checked it matched his paperwork.

The most annoying thing had been the man who had made the bid on behalf of his master. He had insisted on watching the figurines being packed and crated. He had checked the sides, top, and bottom then nodded. Anyone would think

Robert couldn't be trusted!

After the crate was loaded into a van, the Arab's representative climbed in the back and leaned against the crate. After about an hour, they arrived at Stansted airport and made their way to the goods out loading bay. Robert passed the paperwork to an official, who gave a cursory glance toward the crate, stamped a receipt on the paperwork, and called the porter over.

"Take the crate and leave it to the side in the green bay. It's for a private plane, so it needs to be ready for collection and loading once the plane lands."

The porter nodded and disappeared with the crate into the building while the official told Robert to move on. Other vehicles with freight were waiting behind them. The Arab's minion left them to go through customs and security to be ready to board his master's plane once it arrived.

Robert smiled as they left and thought about his next liaison in Dover in the new year. December always was a slow period for the removal business, but his limo business was almost fully booked. He had let one of his removal van drivers take over the limo he'd used, and Roger had taken his partner to Dover to join a P & O cruise over Christmas and New Year. The cruise was to the Caribbean to island hop in the sun.

Business with Partner also dried up over the Christmas period, and into the new year, but once Partner returned, then the resumption of the cruise clients would come about.

CHAPTER TWO

January

Robert had been busy since the last sale with a new warehouse located in Bristol, near the city centre. Others had been offered in Gloucester and Cheltenham.

"Tidy it up, leave no trace of us being there, and move on," his partner always said. "The buyers will like the fact that we're leaving no leads for anyone to follow."

Robert scratched his stomach as he got out of bed. He pulled aside part of the curtains and looked out, expecting to see rain or snow on the windowpane. But no, it was sunny. He shuffled to the kitchen and put the kettle on, then sat munching his morning digestive biscuit. He had stopped dunking; he lost too much of his biscuit in his tea, making it more like porridge.

His thoughts went to his legitimate businesses. His removals team crew packed up everything and load the van, noting the items of interest. Nothing was lost or broken, so the company gained more and more jobs through recommendations. But when there were items of interest, one of his lads would make a copy of the front door key and remember any alarm access codes ready for a visit sometime in the future.

And now, that business was starting to bring in high returns.

Speaking of which, Robert had to get to work. After a short day filled mostly with fielding requests from his clients for new items, Robert closed up the warehouse and got in the limo that was needed for a collection at Dover. This was to do with another business, something that he had a partner with, but this wasn't legitimate. Far from it.

His partner, who was returning from a P & O cruise, had messaged him to make sure he was at the docks with the limo to collect him when his ship arrived. His partner had asked for two tails to be arranged and so Robert, Badger, and John were here at Dover, waiting for him to send the information about the people leaving the ship that they were to follow. One had a location just outside of Brighton, and although no address had been given, the houses in the region were outstanding. The other lived in Rickmansworth, just outside of London: the wealthier people liked to use the Tube from their desirable residence into the capital.

There was no house number on this one, but a road name-dropped in a passing comment gave a slight clue. If nothing else, his partner was always close enough to pick up small bits of info towards the future removals from the owner's home address.

Both owners had told the partner that they lived in detached properties, very handy for what Robert had in mind. At this rate, they should be able to facilitate two black auctions in the coming months.

Robert sat in the car on the jetty, dressed as a chauffeur, waiting for a message or a sign from his partner. It was a miserable dull drab day, and to add to it, the sun had disappeared and the rain had started to fall once again. *No wonder the poor sods go on these cruises. There's bugger all chance of sunshine in good old merry England.*

Robert saw movement at the exit gates as people emerged from the ship and he got out of the car. He glanced around and saw that other drivers were getting ready for their rides. Not that his partner would be first out, but it was important to be seen as one of the many chauffeur drivers waiting for their client.

He shifted from one foot to another as he hunched up against the wind that seemed to have picked up and singled him out for special attention. His phone pinged.

The first one leaving now. She's wearing a dark blue rain mac and a matching hood tied over her hair. Seven cases, all matching light brown in colour. Will be going home in a private limo. Watch for the guy holding a card up with St. Clair on it, or for the loaders to call out for the driver of St. Clair.

A loading steward stepped from his hut and called out, "Tenance and Swanson private hire drivers. Can you drive down to the yellow zone and pick up your passengers, please? The rest of you, please wait."

Two vehicles moved out and down to the area and were soon loading the cases as a couple got in one and a lady in the other.

"St. Clair, Roberts, and Cambridge: your rides are ready to be picked up. Yellow zone, please."

"Mine's St. Clair, so I'll go first," called out a driver as two others followed.

Robert was only interested in his maroon-coloured limo, which would be easy to pick up and follow as it left the docks. Badger was an old hand and a steady driver. Robert messaged Badger with the details, and he promptly replied with a thumbs-up emoji.

Robert watched the maroon car driver load the cases and slam the boot shut before he got into the car. As it pulled away, Robert messaged Badger it was on its way.

Okay, got it governor. See you at base camp.

One down, one to go, thought Robert as the rain increased. He paced up and down as each limo driver was called to pick up their ride.

"Always the same, isn't it?" said a voice behind him, and Robert turned to find a driver wearing a COVID mask had come up close to him.

He frantically pulled on his own mask. "The same as?"

"When you want to make a quick exit, your ride's always the bloody last."

"Mine *will* be the last one; he works on this ship and has just finished his contract."

Just then, a call came from the loading steward.

Drivers for Orbison, Rogers, Caple, and Jamieson, please drive down in that order to the yellow zone to pick up your rides.

The driver turned away. "Got to go, the last one's mine."

Robert felt his phone tingle and looked at the message.

Jamieson. She will have six cases, various colours. She's wearing a brown coat and has a matching handbag. Message once all are tagged and on their way, then I can join you.

Robert took a photo of the registration plate of the black

limo as it passed him then sent it to John. Badger's son wouldn't let him down. He'd proved very useful so far. As the other cars pulled away, he saw the driver of the passenger he was interested in shut the boot and get into the car. Once it pulled away, he messaged John and waited for him to confirm he had picked up the driver. Five minutes later, a message came back stating he was following two cars back and traffic was slow but steady.

Robert messaged his partner, who said he would be with him in about an hour. He had to record his end of duty and go to a debriefing. Robert got back in the limo. No point in getting any wetter. He set the seat back, lay down, and in a short time, he was asleep.

The knocking on the car's window woke him.

A parking steward peered in. "Your ride is waiting; you're the last. Yellow zone, please."

Robert nodded, sorted himself out and then drove down to the yellow zone and parked.

As he got out of the car, he saw his partner pushing a trolley with three suitcases on it.

His partner grinned at him. "Do be careful, Charles, you won't get replacements in a charity shop for those if you damage them."

I could tell you where to put them, and it wouldn't be the car. Robert swung the cases into the boot. "It wouldn't have hurt you to have given me a hand with those cases. One of them was bloody heavy."

"I couldn't be seen helping the help. Most unseemly, old boy."

"Poncy bugger."

"Good-looking poncy bugger, you mean."

Robert grinned at his friend and partner, then started the car and pulled out, manoeuvring past the hordes now getting on the coaches that waited to claim them.

Once they were on the motorway, his partner leaned forward. "How's business?"

"Is this a question to your lackey or your partner?"

"Oh dear. Not in a good mood, are we? Very well, Partner, the question stands. How was business?"

"Just over two hundred thousand. A little extra came in for deliveries. It was a good return."

"We need to increase the jobs. Your removal business helps but only provides a few extra pieces. I'm wondering if it's even worth the risk."

"I have got to keep the lads working until one of our specials comes in. I don't want to lose them between jobs."

"No. Don't end the genuine business—end the odd break in that you arrange after a month or two. It's a free-standing business and above all, legitimate like the chauffeur business."

Robert was quiet for a while then said, "Okay." He glanced at his partner through the rear mirror and watched him sit back. Bringing his eyes back to the road, he concentrated on his driving, slowing slightly as the rain increased, making the windscreen wipers work hard to clear his view of the motorway.

The journey to his partner's house, a small semi-detached house in Surrey, finally ended, and as they arrived, the rain stopped.

This time, his partner helped lift the cases.

Robert pointed at the house. "Might need to mark this gaff down as worthy of a visit on a dark evening when I know that the owner is away."

"I don't think so, mate. Most of the stuff belonged to someone else before."

They both laughed, and as he walked down the drive towards the front door pulling a suitcase, Robert closed the boot and pulled two cases after him muttering about the servants and masters.

When he got to the door, he looked at his partner, and then at the two cases he'd been lugging.

"What? My hands were full, I had a key in one hand and the case in the other. Really. The hired help today is as nothing to what they used to be." He grinned and slapped Robert's shoulder. "Get on home now, my friend, and let me know once you have the addresses of our new clients. We can get together for the next stage in a few days. I have a new booking for a short cruise in a few weeks' time."

As Robert turned, the rain started again. "Typical." He pulled his collar up to shield his neck as the rain started to pick on him again, and he made his way back up the drive.

He cast his mind back to his partner and the story he'd told him how he got on the "other side" of the fence-working.

He was, he'd been told, a university graduate in law, of all things. He was good-looking, his face unmarked by any fist, unlike Robert. His nails were always clean, and his hair was always trimmed and styled with a small wave at the front. Nothing about him was unpleasant to look at. Robert had seen him whisking a young lady around the dance floor at the lord mayor's ball. His partner had booked one of Robert's limos and that was how they had met. No doubt about it, everything he did was an indication of a monied lifestyle.

He was well-spoken, not with a plum in his mouth, but close. His family had been disappointed that he'd failed to follow his father into gowns and silks and eventually up to a judge. Instead, their son had left the country and travelled around the world, meeting people and pressing the palms of others who had passed through university with him or close to him.

Once he returned, he worked on behalf of a friend in one of the Arab states, bidding and buying various paintings, vases, and other art collections and arranging for transport to his buyer. His retainer was very healthy, but when his father had cut off his allowance, apparently to bring him to his senses, he turned his back on the old man and dug in his heels.

The story from his partner then got mega interesting.

It had been while he was looking at a miniature Dutch oil painting for his Arab client that was coming up in a forthcoming auction sale when he'd overheard the owner say, "I do hope it reaches the asking price. I shall have to sell another one to meet the death duty otherwise. It would have been better if they'd been stolen, then the treasury wouldn't have any need for their pound of flesh."

As the agent and the lady moved away, he'd been struck with an idea. He could oblige the lady and make a great deal of money into the bargain. He looked at the catalogue, saw the minimum offered price, and his life on the other side of the law started.

It had been a little difficult to find out the lady's address but after a few days, and a fifty-pound bribe, he'd secured it. He had sounded out Robert, asking if he had any contacts in the business of removing items from people who might not necessarily like them removing. Robert said he could help, and the alliance began. His partner left the arrangements to him.

The house had been a detached property, standing on a couple of acres of ground. A van with a fabricated electrical repair company name arrived and parked across the drive. They cut the supply of electricity to the house and the phone line. Wearing a mask because of COVID, Robert had walked down the driveway and knocked on the door. He explained to the lady that they needed access to her home to restore the electricity but it would be at no cost to her. Trusting his honest appearance, she had opened the door.

Robert entered, left the door ajar, and let the lady lead him through the house, holding a small implement with a red bulb on its end. He touched various sockets and shook his head, and the lady followed him around.

Unknown to the lady, his two associates had followed him into the house and gone upstairs. Moving from room to room, with the lady following, he ended up in the kitchen. He watched as his two lads quietly left, giving him the thumbs up. "Thank you for your help. I've isolated the fault, and you'll soon be back to normal."

At the door, the lady complained about COVID and how it had ruined her social life.

Robert had agreed. "This mask makes me look like a bandit, but it's for your safety, as you know." He then walked up the drive and closed the gate behind him.

He got back in the van and peeled off his thin rubber gloves. "Did you find it? It wasn't in the lounge or any room downstairs."

Badger had laughed. "We got all three. There must have been four going up the stairs. We could see the marks of the one that'd been removed for sale. As we had a bit of extra time, we picked up a few other bits: a watch, and two old-fashioned necklaces that were laying around."

The new partnership had done well from that, and a new venture had started.

It had been his partner who had come up with the idea of lining up people who were on their own after the three oil paintings were sold privately to his buyer who had told him to bid for the other one in the auction. The lady got the amount she had wanted, and his partner felt happy he had helped the poor woman, assuaging his conscience.

It had been plain to them both that a chance meeting was no good. It had to be organised. How to find wealthy widows just waiting to make donations to the poor was the problem.

Three weeks later, Robert had had another visit. His partner laid out the scheme, with his part costing nothing to the company, and they decided to give it a try. John had said that they would get more if they sold on the dark web. He'd explained how it worked, and then set up a site for them to see.

After several tests from different locations, they agreed the next lot would be listed as a black auction with a secret location. The money grew as a result and now they always had the black auctions. The main players would meet in a pub, again never the same one, and go over the list of names and addresses the partner had provided. If he hadn't gotten the full address, then they would follow the ones that the partner pointed out and get the exact address.

Then at the meeting, the partner would ask for the address of Mrs. Jones of Somewhere, and this would be added to the growing list. His partner would have a date when the lady was next going on a cruise and to where, and he would find out what ship.

On the day for boarding, one of the crew would follow the pick-up car to the docks, watch the cases put onto a trolley, and then make sure the lady boarded. Once the ship sailed, the house was raided within two or three days, with anything that had been mentioned in passing listed for special attention. For a lot of the removals, his partner had found out the full address, which he mailed to Robert, and the removal was arranged very quickly.

The business went on growing, and so did the profits.

Robert knew his name, but his partner insisted that he should only be called Partner in front of any of the crew. Robert also knew why his partner wanted it this way, but if things went badly, he also knew where he lived and who his parents were. Insurance should always be considered in any venture.

But Robert had an inkling that something wasn't quite right.

He had asked himself many questions. Why should the partner insist on using the word partner instead of a false name as a way to address him? But it wasn't just that. It was something else, and Robert kept it at the back of his mind fermenting, waiting for a glimmer of an idea to come forth.

Two weeks later, Robert drove his partner down to Dover and watched him board one of the cruise ships.

Eight days later, his partner messaged that he hadn't found out any prospects from the people onboard.

CHAPTER THREE

February

Anyone who casually observed the four people sitting in the pub's restaurant area ordering their meal might think it was a business meeting. Not that many people were in the pub's restaurant area anyway. The day had been carefully chosen, and the few people in the restaurant confirmed that a Tuesday lunch was a quiet time for the pub.

Such meetings occur up and down the country, and to some extent, it *was* a business meeting. One man was dressed in a suit, a white shirt, and a tie. He had the sort of good looks that caused women to stare. His companion wore a dark blue blazer, a blue shirt open at the neck, and grey trousers. The other two men sitting with them wore jeans and check shirts. Their jackets, now on the back of the chairs, were charcoal grey and well-worn.

"First the Brighton client, Lucinda St. Clair. We now have her full address," said the smart gent with the tie. He looked at his notes. "I can tell you that she's due to sail again next month to the Caribbean for twenty-one days. She told me she sails from Southampton, and I think it will be the Royal Caribbean line. We'll need you to check this out, Robert. Date of sailing unknown, but it shouldn't be too hard to find out."

"Any tips from her about any of her special interests?" asked Robert.

"Yes. She said she always worries about her late husband's gold coin collection when she goes away."

"Any clue as to where this collection maybe?"

"I'm afraid not, Robert. I don't press our clients; it might raise suspicion."

"So, a search and find sort of job. I think this one will need a little more planning before we go in," said Robert. He turned to Badger. "Was there a driveway at the house? And could we get the van down it without any nosey parkers seeing us?"

"No problem about that, boss. The whole of the front is bordered by a high hedge. It's a drive in one way and out the other."

Robert turned back to his partner. "Smacks of money, Partner. We must give it special attention when we visit. I will drop down and have a look-see. If there's an alarm, I'll check if it has a link to the local cop shop. Nice of these alarm installers to tell us the type they fitted. So helpful."

The meals arrived and as the server placed the meals in front of the customers, other than appreciative comments about the food, no more was said.

Badger drank a sip of the beer. "To business," he said and raised his glass. Each clinked their glasses and settled to eat the meal, the discussion put in abeyance for the moment.

Once the meal was concluded and their plates removed, Robert asked the waitress if they could have a short time to relax before they looked at the dessert menu.

The server left and their partner said, "Well now, after that exceptionally nice meal, shall we continue? The Rickmansworth client, Louise Jamieson. Who followed her?"

"I did," said John.

"Okay. What can you tell us about this one?"

"She's got a four-bedroom house with a large garden. I checked the local estate agents, and a similar property is under offer in the next road." He checked his notes. "The front of the house has a low wall bordering the pavement outside. It'd be hard to avoid being noticed from the outside. Nice kept garden, flowers and low bushes dotted around. Looked like the place was alarmed. When she went in, she left the door open, and the limo driver stood outside with the cases. There are two cameras on the outside wall and there could be more that I couldn't see. It looked like a wealthy area. Most of the houses had cameras and I also saw one of the dreaded signs: Neighbourhood watch area."

"Did you try to go around the back? Is there any route that way?"

"I drove out of the road and parked away from our client's

house, then pulled my hat on, added specs, and put on the long coat that I wear to change my shape. That cushion sewn into it makes me look nice and fat. I took my walking stick and walked the whole of the cul-de-sac. I found a lane between eighteen and nineteen that went between the houses, and that brought me to a field. Kids were playing football and there were plenty of dog walkers. I stopped and then worked out where the house was and looked over a wooden fence. From what I could see, no cameras were at the back."

"You did well, John. If we do go into this house, we're going to need to gain entry from the rear, disable the alarm, and go out the front way."

"Well, I may have an answer to that. If we could get a look-a-like council lorry and drive into the field, we may then be able to load up from the back and leave the field the same way. I walked across to the gate, and it was well-used by the council. They must cut the grass on a regular basis. The gate comes out onto the next road."

"For a moment I thought we would have to draw a line under this one, but thanks to you, John," Partner pointed at John, "I think it's worth looking into. Don't you, Robert?"

"Yes, I do." Robert looked at John. "Was the gate to the field padlocked?"

"Yes, but it's a cheap and nasty one. The cutters will open that in seconds."

Robert smiled. "Council cutbacks, don't you just love them?"

"John, do you think you could get your friend Billy Drayton to do the alarm once again? Tell him the usual cash fee. Stress to him that it's a mask and rubber glove job. No fingerprints to be left."

"I'll contact him when we return."

"Any clues about the items she's concerned about?"

"Afraid not, but she was always well-dressed, had a high opinion of herself, and wasn't afraid to express it. I'd just love to shock this one. I've been told that she hopes her next cruise will be better than the last one, because there were so many common people on it. She leaves with P & O in five months."

Partner took on the voice of a posh woman. "Sailing from Liverpool, a most inconvenient port of embarkation, but I have arranged for a limousine to convey me to the port. It is better to arrive in comfort than to arrive by coach. I saw you arrive by limousine and board. I am sure you will agree."

Everyone laughed.

"Okay, it's another seek and find job," said Robert. "We know roughly when she's due to leave, so we can check the P & O schedules and find out the exact date. Any idea where she's going?"

"Oh, yes, sorry. She's going to Canada and America for twenty-nine days." Partner looked at everyone sitting at the table. "Any other business?" After no one responded, he said, "Meeting closed. Please keep me posted about the jobs in hand, Robert. On my next cruise, I'm going to the Mediterranean and the islands. The furthest point is Bosnia and Herzegovina, into Gibraltar on the return leg then return to Southampton. Ray Butler is also going, and as I've told you before, he's a very good friend of mine that I met on one of the past cruises. When you're taken on as staff, you never know who's going to be sleeping in the cabin with you. Having worked with Sting Ray, I've asked to bunk in with him."

"So, I suppose you'll want to be treated like royalty and arrive in a limousine again, captain?"

"Of course, it's appropriate to my appearance, and it's important to impress the rest of the staff and passengers who might notice."

"I know. But do I have to wear the monkey suit? It's so demeaning."

"Yes, Robert. If you're part of the play, then you take the part wholeheartedly. It's surprising how many people notice that I arrive in a limo with my chauffeur. It's a great ice-breaker and helps establish that I'm a wealthy type with no interest in other people's money."

"Don't you get asked why you do this job? After all, if you've got lots of lolly, why would you?" asked John.

"Good question," said Partner as he stood and pulled on his topcoat. "I get asked that a lot. My answer is always the same. I get bored sitting at home alone in my house. I do this job, not for the money, but because I get the chance to dine with so many new faces who have so many interesting stories to tell."

Badger asked, "You said you like to mix with people; do you use that to find our clients?"

"Yes. But I also find out if anyone has any future cruise plans and if they're taking up the discount for onboard future bookings. Then, once they say they intend to do that, I try to bump into them accidentally once I know their appointment time, and I listen to their postcodes and first line of address. That tells me where they live. All I need then is the next date of sailing."

He shook each of his fellow diner's hands and went over to the bar and paid cash for the meal—cards would leave a trail. When he returned, he picked up the part-used bottle of wine and led the group out. "Waste not, want not," he said as he held the bottle to his side.

Once outside, Badger and John went to their vehicle, Robert asked, "Who is the cruise line this time?"

"Fred Olsen. I haven't sailed with them before. They run smaller ships, a bit like Saga. It'll be interesting to see what this cruise brings."

Robert watched as his partner got into a small run-around car and drove off.

That itch came again, and one of these days, he would get to scratch it. Something was definitely out of kilter between him and his partner, but what?

CHAPTER FOUR

March

T ime had passed quite quickly after their last meeting, and on a dry but blustery day, Robert watched his partner board the cruise ship that would take him away for just over three weeks. He unloaded Partner's suitcases from the boot of the limo and placed them onto a trolley to be whisked away to his partner's cabin.

The porter, having stood and watched Robert unload the car and place the cases onto the hand cart, offered no help. "Is that the lot?" he asked.

Robert nodded, and the porter pushed the trolley away. Robert shut the boot, got back into the car, and pulled the limousine out, passing other vehicles waiting to empty their passengers and luggage. He had a steady run back to Surrey and then a group meeting to arrange the next legitimate removal job ahead of him. This side of his business had taken a dive with the outbreak of COVID, but now people were starting to want to move again.

Making sure he didn't go over the speed limit, he still made good time back to his legitimate business and went upstairs to his living quarters above the storeroom. The warehouse was big enough for three removal vans and at a push, the truck that was used for some more awkward-sized loads. It also had a toilet and a tea-making area for his crew to sit and take a break. A small box room was used occasionally by his ex-lady friend who came in to take the phone calls for legitimate bookings.

He'd just changed out of the chauffeur's suit and put on the kettle when someone knocked on the door.

He walked to the door with his cup in his hand and a teabag in the other. "Who is it?"

"It's Badger, boss. I know you just got back, but I think you need to hear this bit of news."

"Come in, Badger. I'm making a cupper. If you want one,

grab a cup and sort one out for yourself. I'm desperate for a strong brew." Uniting the tea bag with the cup, he poured hot water into the cup and gave it a vigorous stir. The flavour was going to come out, like it or not.

Badger soon joined his boss and placed his mug of tea carefully on a cork mat, aware that Robert was fussy about that sort of thing.

Robert took a sip of the scalding liquid and replaced his mug. "Well, come on, Badger. What's bothering you?"

"Well, you remember Alan Harding? He got done for trying to pawn his sister-in-law's necklace. Yesterday, he dropped by and asked if we had any jobs coming up. He's just come out of the nick, and no one will take him on. I told him we had no vacancies at the moment but that I'd talk to you when you got back."

"Well, Badger, I'm glad you said you'd have a chat with me, but I don't want someone who would stoop so low to half-inch from kith and kin. As I remember, his brother Troy was well annoyed and put him in hospital before the cops nicked him. No, Badger. We honest villains must live by our unwritten code, and we don't want to get a bad name now we're so squeaky clean. I'll let Troy know that we've been approached but won't be offering him a job, as we're only interested in our two legitimate companies."

Badger nodded. "John has the details about the date of sailing for our Brighton client. Mrs St. Clair should be boarding the Royal Caribbean line at Southampton to travel to the Caribbean next Saturday. She'll be gone for twenty-one days, and once we check she boards the ship, we can schedule our visit."

"Excellent news, Badger. Tell John he did well. Has he lined up his mate Billy Drayton to do his magic on the alarms?"

"Yep. John said he'll let him know when, and Billy will bring his box of tricks."

"We need to put an eye on our client, make sure she sails, and then book our visit."

"The Rickmansworth removal is going to take longer. We've got the date of her sailing, but it's quite a while before that happens."

"We can leave her in our pending file for now. Partner is on his way today and will be trying to message about any possible clients as he sails the seven seas. Now for the legitimate removals. I've agreed that we can do a removal from France to Oxford. They want four vans all at the same time. I've sounded out the Wall to link up with his two vans. We'll need to sort out a price for the job with him."

He continued, "Adrian's worked with us before, so we'll work out a price and split it fifty-fifty. We don't want to ruin a good job by being greedy. We couldn't do it without his help, so we let him join in on the negotiation for the price."

"Okay, boss." Badger finished his tea and left.

Robert sat back and lifted his feet up onto the stool at the side of his desk. *A nice legitimate job that French removal.* He closed his eyes and drifted off to sleep with thoughts of money, which always relaxed Priceright.

***

Eight days had passed when the proposed visit to Brighton became a possibility. John had observed Mrs. St. Clair get into a small multi-people carrier, joining two other people already in the vehicle. The same seven matching cases, light brown in colour were loaded into the back as she climbed into the front.

John had followed the multi-carrier to Southampton and watched her suitcases being unloaded from the back of the vehicle. The other occupants and their client walked to the check-in.

John had waited until the vehicle had left, then returned to base to report that their client had vacated the property and was ready for the removal job whenever they were ready. Robert had also got in touch with Troy Harding and then visited him. He told him about the request for a job from his brother Alan and explained that he wouldn't be offering him a job because he was running a legitimate company now and couldn't risk getting a bad name if his brother half-inched a few items to sell.

Troy was quite happy about it, thanked Priceright, and said he would see his brother and mark his card. Robert had shuddered; he wouldn't want to have his card marked by the towering block of muscle standing in front of him. He bruised so easily!

He was about to sit down at his desk when his mobile phone pinged. It was Partner with some interesting news. Working with his friend, who had no idea that he was gleaning information for nefarious means, he had been able to get an address for a client on board the Fred Olsen boat. It would need a little work but half a day watching three houses was no problem.

No info about items that would be available but knowing that their future client wouldn't be back for a while gave the team time to do a full search. It would involve a run along the south coast back to Southampton, but once the house number was established and the area located, this removal could be worked in well.

Robert sat at his desk and opened his working diary for crew one. He studied the forthcoming bookings for the legitimate removals, noting the three-day booking for both of his removal vans to go across to France. Ferry costs and bookings had been taken care of. They would then drive to Brittany to the old mansion house to partly load. Loading should finish the next day, then they'd catch the ferry back to Dover and travel to Oxford. Finally, the following morning, they would start unloading each van into a warehouse on the land where a new house was being built. Adrian (nicknamed the Wall after Hadrian's wall) and Robert had worked out their costs for the three days, added on the 20% profit, and both were pleased to have the 50% transferred into the bank.

Robert had transferred half into Adrian's bank account, and they had agreed that the vans wouldn't be unloaded in Oxford until the client paid the balance.

"Mustn't take chances on them not paying," he had said. "Far too many criminals out there trying to rip us honest businessmen off."

There was a three-day gap before then, and Robert pencilled in the Southampton job as a night job. Next, he looked at dates after the Oxford job and pencilled in another night job. St. Clair, with a crescent moon by it, was his indicator for the other side of his business.

He closed the diary and went to find Badger.

The second crew were out working on a job moving stock for a client who had bought out everything from a failed business in London. It was a simple collection and delivery up to Birmingham. It pleased Robert that this crew could be totally legitimate *and* profitably busy.

He employed Sandra, a lady who had graced his bed on a few occasions before she got too serious. Now she had a steady relationship with a rugby player. She had no dealings with crew two's night work, but Robert always told her to not book anything on the day the night job came up. He told her they were booked in to remove staging from a show, and it was an evening and night job. Other than those night bookings, she would try to get bookings for the two removal vans. Robert was pleased that she just accepted that and never asked how he got the booking.

He gave her the dates for the night jobs, and she wrote it down.

"These pop singers have a lot of gear to move around. Good job I have a mate in the business who rings me."

That should alleviate any doubts you might have in your mind, Sandra, was his passing thought as he went to find Badger, who he told to inform the lads that a night job was coming up in Southampton, and Robert gave him the date. He reminded Badger that he should tell John to pick up his wizard Billy for the alarms. He would be with them when they went because he liked to keep an eye on them.

CHAPTER FIVE

March

Dubrovnik looked lovely to the two ladies as they leaned on the balcony rail and watched the ship they were on manoeuvre into its position next to the dock.

The pink and white painted houses with terracotta tiled roofs climbed up the side of the steep hill in front of them, clinging to the edge of the hill. Against the rich greens of the trees and shrubs clinging to the rock, they could see a strong magenta colour from the bougainvillea competing for space. The noise of traffic from the road near the ship was the only thing that spoiled this idyllic setting.

Gill looked at a roofless house just outside the dock. "A desirable residence, but it needs some modernising."

Sheila laughed as she looked at the house in question. Neither of them were interested in that sort of venture, but it was the sort of close humour the friends shared. They'd met on a cruise and both their husbands and the ladies seemed to gel. Other holidays followed, and all went well until Gill's husband died.

This could have torn them apart but grief-stricken, they had attended the funeral. Sheila and Graham consoled Gill and her two daughters, but words can never be enough at times like that. The usual platitude of "We'll keep in touch" were exchanged, but this time, unlike so many others, they had done exactly that while Sheila and Graham continued their cruising.

Tragedy came for Sheila eighteen months later when a visit from the police informed her that her husband had been killed in a car accident. Once again, the ladies met, this time in reversed circumstances.

They'd talked again after the funeral, and Gill persuaded Sheila to consider going on a cruise with her sometime in the future. Her son Robin, who lived in Australia, urged her to give it some consideration. It took some time before she agreed, but here they were on their fifth or sixth cruise together.

They were booked on a guided tour and as they watched, a coach arrived and parked next to the ship. This was closely followed by another.

"Time we sorted ourselves out before the tour. Mustn't be tardy on the boarding of the coach," said Gill as they retreated to their cabin.

The tour took them around the old town and then up into the mountains, where they could look down on the road bridge they had gone over and could see their cruise ship anchored in the dock, looking like a toy boat. The tour was as expected: a delightful mixture of short stops with views of a scenic nature or a visit to an artisan venture. Pottery, lace making, and even a taste of wine all made the package a great success.

They returned to the ship and freshened up.

Gillian Blakeney (who preferred to be called Gill) changed into her charcoal-coloured dress and stood in front of the mirror, checking to see if anything looked out of place. She was a tall and elegant, straight-backed lady, slightly thin to an observer's eye, but one would have trouble guessing her age by just her poise and her ready smile. She was a lady who took trouble over her looks, as could be discerned by her dress sense. One could say she dressed in a modest elegance, and most times welcomed an approach by anyone with a smile.

At five feet eight, no one should be fooled into thinking Gill was a pushover. She was always observing all around her, assessing and storing information. Gill had the ability to tune into any conversation going on within her sharp hearing and block out any other unwanted conversation. She liked to dance with the host dancers on any cruise, and any others who might offer. She wore costume jewellery and also had the real thing. She wasn't pretentious and could dress up or down for any occasion.

Sheila Chancel was shorter and younger than Gill and slightly thicker set, but the dancing was equally important to her. Her dress sense was like her demeanour, quieter tones, stylish, and classic. Still holding her figure, she was a woman who men would notice when she entered a room. Sheila wasn't one to push to the front of the queue; she knew she would get there sometime, so why rush? It's true that she would mostly defer to her friend, but what one wanted invariably matched the other's wish, or somewhere near to it. She liked her diamonds, pearls, and opals, and those gems complemented her dress on special occasions.

On approaching someone new, her eyes will roll up to the face of the person and then, having assessed them, her face will light up. An observer might feel that this lady had had a rough time of it, but if that was true then the result was hidden beneath the surface, for no mention was made about it in any conversation.

Both ladies liked a bottle of red wine and would work through the evenings topping up their glasses until several bottles were ready to recycle. Mixing with all types of people gave the ladies new perspectives, some pleasant, some that should be quickly forgotten. Any amorous attentions were quickly dispelled. They shared the dining table with other single ladies. Ladies only was not by choice, but because the overwhelming majority of ladies were in the same position as they were and had a common ground to start with, and they all seemed to rub along reasonably well.

Conversation on this evening was mostly about the tours they had gone on, and all but one of the eight at the table were vocal in their praise or voiced disappointment of something that had not reached expectations.

Gill turned to Sheila and whispered, "Martina seems very subdued this evening. I wonder if something has upset her. Could you ask her? It might be that she's had some bad news from her family… An illness, or something like that."

"Good idea." Sheila turned to Martina and gently asked the question.

Martina shook her head and sighed. "My daughter rang to inform me that my house was broken into yesterday, and they took everything. All of my valuables and my jewellery, and even my furniture. The two bronze statues left to my husband by his mother, and then to me, are gone. They're insured, of course, but they were so special and reminded me of Barry. I'm so upset. Why do people do that sort of thing?"

"Look. Eat your meal. Pushing it around the plate isn't going to help. Once we can excuse ourselves, join Gill and me for a drink, and you can talk it through with us. It won't solve your problem but talking about it might lessen the pain."

Martina nodded but continued to play with her food a little more before giving up altogether.

"Come on," said Sheila. "Let's go somewhere else a little quieter, and we can talk."

She put her knife and fork onto her plate and stood. "If you'll excuse me, ladies, Martina isn't feeling very well, so I'm going to take her back to her cabin."

Mutterings of "I hope it's not COVID," brought a frown to a few others at the table, who leaned away from Martina just in case. As if that would help.

Sheila whispered to Gill, "Observation room." She took Martina's arm and led her out of the dining room to the observation room, which was always quiet while the dinner service was on.

They found a table away from the odd few people in the room, and Gill soon joined them. "I find it helps to talk about these things. It doesn't sort it out, but it helps if someone's there to listen."

Sheila told Gill what the problem was, and they both focused their attention on Martina.

Martina took a deep breath. "My neighbour Brenda noticed the front door to my house was ajar. She calls around to water my pot plants. They'd busted the door, disabled the alarm, and helped themselves. Brenda rang Susan, my daughter, and she went to the house and confirmed that I'd been burgled."

A waitress hovered near to the ladies, and Gill said, "Why don't we have a glass of wine as you gather your thoughts, then if you wish, you can tell us what else was taken."

With a glass of red wine, and each having a sip in support for Martina, the sorry story continued.

"It would seem that these were very professional thieves.

Susan said the police thought this was an organised group, targeting single people. When she asked how they would know I was now a widow, they said that thieves kept their eyes on social media and notices of death." She took another sip and shook her head. "They took anything that had an intrinsic value. My collection of miniature silver love spoons and plates that we had collected from around the world. No great value as a single unit, but as a collection, was insured for a few hundred pounds. It's so unsettling. When Barry was alive, we used to go to the 1940s weekend, me dressed in a 40s dress and he in a sailor's costume, or an air force, or army costume. All those clothes are gone. Then the two paintings by Alwyn Crawshaw that we bought in Cornwall. He wasn't a well-known artist back when we purchased them, but they're sought after now. There'll be other things, I'm sure, but those are some of the items my son could see were missing and told the police about."

"Unfortunately, that seems to be one of the risks we take leaving our home for a holiday, even with a partner or on our own, as we are. It's random, but it happens," said Sheila.

"I thought that," said Martina, "but then you start to wonder about the taxi driver. Could he have informed the thieves that I would be away for two weeks? It's so unsettling."

"Have you used the taxi driver before?" asked Gill.

"Oh, yes. He's local to us. He drove us to Southampton a few times when Barry and I went cruising."

"I don't think he'd have anything to do with it then, do you?" said Gill.

"No. You're probably right, but I'm so angry. I feel so abused. How could this happen to me?" Martina wiped her eyes and looked at the two ladies. "Thank you both. I knew I was going to explode at any moment as I listened to the mundane commentary about their day. When you asked if I was okay, I realised someone had actually noticed something was wrong. Thank you."

Gill smiled and patted Martina's knee. "Are the police making the house secure?"

"No, my son is going to get someone in to fit a new lock or a new door once the police have finished doing whatever they need to do. Once I get back, I'll have to go through the house and list everything that has gone."

"You do have insurance, I assume," said Sheila.

"Yes, but money isn't going to bring back the things that stimulated my memories."

Sheila grimaced. "No, it isn't."

They sat for a moment, and then Sheila said, "The most important thing to remember is that they can steal your things, but no one can take your memories away from you. When I first spoke to you, I wondered if someone in your family had been rushed into hospital. This is awful, but you'll move on from it."

Martina shrugged. "Yes, I see what you're saying, but I can't get the thought out of my mind of those people going through the clothes drawers, handling my knickers. I shall put everything in the washing machine once I get home."

Both of the ladies laughed, and Martina couldn't help but join in.

They stayed with her until the entertainment started, then said they were going down to a lower deck to see if they could get a dance with one of the hosts.

Martina said she would go back to her cabin, thanked the two ladies and after she'd walked away, Gill and Sheila took the lift to the fifth deck to join in on the dancing provided.

They felt that they were very fortunate on this cruise. Most of the time, the dance hosts would be poor to average dancers, but there were extremely proficient dancers on this cruise. It was a joy to dance with a man who could whisk the ladies around the floor. The problem was that with so many of the ladies in the same position as they were, the hosts had to share their time with many eager dancers. And there was always some who would be disappointed. But getting a little dancing was better than none.

It was much later when they were in their cabin getting ready for bed that the subject of the robbery came up.

"Poor Martina," said Sheila as she took her dress off and hung it on a hanger. "This has ruined the joy of the holiday for her. All she's going to do now is go over all the things she had of value in the house. I don't know how I would start on something like that."

Gill called out from the bathroom, "No, nor can I. You don't go around making a list of items, do you? You accept that you have them and that they hold a memory. I don't envy her on this. I won't be long. I'm just going to clean my teeth then the bathroom's all yours."

Sheila sat on her bed, thinking about Martina.

It had been a long day and a good one for both of them but certainly not for their dining partner, Martina.

CHAPTER SIX

March / April

Robert sat back in his favourite chair and let his mind wander over the new items that they had for the next black action from their latest clients, Martina Kincade and Lucinda St. Clair.

The house in Southampton had been relatively easy to get in. They had to force the front door, and although there was an alarm, it hadn't been working. Robert had still paid Billy Drayton the extra, although he did hate to do so for nothing. Still, he'd been an extra willing hand moving things into the van.

And what they'd found on this visit would more than compensate for that small loss. The collection of silver miniature love spoons would stir interest, and the ones made from the Welsh mines would lift the price a little more. Robert hadn't rated the set of plates that they'd found, but subsequent online research had changed his mind. That daft sod Badger had lifted a load of old togs that looked like they were from the 1940s, saying they were well sought after, even though Robert had told him he was wasting his time. Priceright was proven wrong, and in a private sale, all of them had gone up to Carlisle to a retro shop and raised £200. Better still, they'd sent a guy down to Slough to collect it all, so there'd been no extra cost to them. He'd arranged to meet in the Herschel Arms in Slough to ensure there was no crossover with his legitimate business. The buyer knew the Irish pub and had no trouble arriving there. Thinking about it, maybe he should have asked for more.

The two bronze statues were interesting, and because they were antique, they'd fetch a tidy sum. Then his mind turned to the rectangular mahogany Georgian tilt top dining table, quad legs with castors, and six chairs, all with the bow front legs and straight-backed rear legs. The seats had been newly replaced with antique-looking green upholstery, and

Priceright didn't think the price would be lowered very much because of this. He would ask for £1000 and see where it went from there.

The two paintings by Alwyn Crawshaw, the Cornish artist could be a problem. Time was when you could pick up a painting of his for £100, but now, you could add a nought to it. The trouble is, the people who came to the auction, wouldn't buy them to hide; they'd want to sell them on. Anyone who bought these couldn't sell them on to any legitimate buyers; those sort of people have a habit of displaying lower-priced paintings on their walls, and that might bring an unwanted question about them. It only wanted one eagle-eyed guest to enquire where they got it, and problems started.

TVs could get sold on easily, so they always took them. They weren't worth a lot, but it all added up. The necklaces, rings, and bracelets would be broken up and the gold melted down, while the jewels would be mounted into other jewellery. A couple of porcelain figurines would be put aside, and as others came in, they'd be added to it to make a job lot.

He remembered the last mixture he offered of assorted toby jugs. Again, it wasn't something Robert could understand people wanting, but if collectors wanted the ugly things, who was he to disappoint them? Then there was the Chinese wall mounting painted on bamboo and silk. A masterpiece indeed. They'd nearly missed it, but it caught Robert's eye after he'd passed it two or three times. Having looked at others like it, he estimated its worth at £5,000.

After three days of working on the France to Oxford booking, their client Lucinda St. Clair had a visit. Lucinda. What a stupid name to call a woman. What was wrong with Lucy? When they arrived, Billy had run down the road, opened the gate, and they drove the van to the door. Again, the weather had been kind, and although it was very windy, not a drop of rain had fallen on the team.

The lock had taken a little longer than expected, but once Billy was in and had attached his gizmo to the alarm, he wiped the recorded footage of their arrival and replayed the previous footage on a loop. The gold coins had been a problem, but when they found a safe that was bolted to the floor, they cut the floorboards, lifted the safe, and took it to the van. It would have been better to have got a more expensive safe, bolted to the concrete floor, but fortunately, people like to cut down on costs.

Not very much else had been of interest. A few porcelain figures, three early handbags that Badger knew had value. A Grandmother clock, but they left that when they saw the woodworm in it. They only wanted quality items to sell on, not firewood! There was a radio and CD player, but no TV. They decided to leave these for the old lady to take some comfort in when she came home to an otherwise empty house. There were some silver items, a watch, and some odd-looking tribal art that they had no idea if it had any value but took it anyway.

Marks on the wall from pictures showed their own story; their client wasn't doing as well as she liked to advertise. She'd obviously been selling them to pay for all her cruises. *I hope the old girl has got everything insured, then she can get the cash for another cruise.*

All in all, it wasn't a bad haul, although they still needed to open the safe.

And there was still one client to visit, a sticky one it had to be acknowledged, but with careful planning, the Jamieson woman's house would be cleaned before her return.

Robert sat and went through the bookings for genuine removals and thought how well this business was going. Perhaps he should give thought to buying another van. The limousine business was also doing well. With two vehicles, they had bookings for quite a few days with each driver. It covered their costs and garnered a small profit.

A few moments later, Badger knocked and walked into the office. "You're not going to believe this, boss. We got the safe open, and there's nothing in it. All that bloody lifting and sweating for nothing."

"You're joking, Badger, aren't you?"

"No, boss. All the trays with info on each coin are there, but that's it."

"The crafty sneaky cow! She wanted to be burgled. She got rid of the coins, then dropped a few words here and there in the hope that honest burglars like us would help her with the insurance. She gets paid twice."

"What shall I do about the safe then, boss?"

"I suppose it won't work now?"

"No, it's useless."

"Drop it down to Crusher Harris and ask him to put it in the back of the next car he scraps. It's getting to something when a poor removal man gets outsmarted by a little old lady. Let that be a lesson to you, Badger," he said, waggling his finger. "Trust no one."

Badger grinned. "I wonder if the old girl suspected that someone on the boat was looking out for rich old birds to rob. Makes you wonder, boss, doesn't it?"

"Oh, Badger, don't even go there. You'll give me an ulcer. Now get on with the honest side of the business, and remember, in just over two months we have an appointment with the Jamieson house.

CHAPTER SEVEN

April / May

Just over four weeks later, Partner and Robert were sitting in Robert's living quarters over the removal storeroom. Robert studied Partner as he sat reading the lists of items and the estimates of value. And there it was again, that itch. What was it that caused Robert to question the validity of Partner?

Even when he was dressed casually, Partner looked as if he had stepped out of an advert for posh casual apparel. His trousers had a crease in them that looked like it could slice up a pizza. His shirt still had fold marks in it as if it had just come out of a package, and the jacket that he had slung on the back of one of the chairs at the table had a tailor-made label. And who the hell polishes their shoes so that the reflection of the ceiling can be seen in them? He had even flicked the chair with his unused hanky to clear any dust from it before he sat. Poncy bugger!

Partner placed the sheets down on the small table beside him and smiled at Priceright. "Robert, you and the boys have done well. If we get near to those estimates, I shall be very pleased."

"Our Rickmansworth client came through very strongly, but that crafty codger St. Clair stitched us up."

"Yes, most annoying, Robert, but we must be prepared to win some and lose some in this game. Overall, we've come up trumps."

Robert nodded and asked how Martina Kincade had divulged so much information. Partner explained that during casual conversation as he or Sting Ray had danced with a single lady by the name of Martina, he'd found out that she had a home just outside of Southampton. By looking up some roads and saying to her as they danced, "I don't suppose your house is near Gurney Road, where a friend of mine lives," he found out the road name she lived in. He had then worked on the number, by talking about the cabin numbers, and how no cabin had a thirteen on any deck. He had said it wouldn't bother him to live in number thirteen, but he could understand those who were superstitious.

She had smiled as he whisked her around the floor. "I live next door to number thirteen, and Brenda, my neighbour who does live in number thirteen, isn't bothered at all about it. She waters my plants while I'm away."

So, it only needed someone to park down outside number thirteen and see if people were moving around in number eleven or fifteen, to find the house that was owned by Martina Kincade. John had done that, proving his usefulness once again. He watched the old lady come from number thirteen, go into number eleven and water the plants. Number fifteen had people coming and going, so eleven had to be the client's house for the scheduled removal visit.

Partner relooked at the list. "When are you going to organise the next black sale?"

"It's already arranged. I've booked our next warehouse in Bristol. Plenty of parking and a good one week's rental price. John has uploaded the items and we've already had quite a lot of interest so far."

Partner read through the list and the estimated values once more. "The four matching vases will sell well. Doulton always does, but four should push the asking price up even more." He adjusted his position in the chair. "The Chinese wall mounting was a good find. I contacted my Arab friend, and he's offered six thousand based on my estimate. He particularly liked the idea that it was painted on bamboo and silk."

"We still auction it, and the highest bidder gets it," said Robert, unwilling to take the chance of losing additional potential profit.

"Yes, he knows that, but that was his offer. You still start it at five thousand. Well, Robert, I must be going. Lots to do before my next voyage." He stood and put his hand on Robert's shoulder. "You've done well, my friend. We can only hope the next auction brings us a higher return than last time."

***

Gill and Sheila had decided to get together to talk about booking another cruise. It was agreed that Sheila would come to Gill's temporary home. Temporary, because she'd made an offer for a house further down the road. She wanted a bigger garden, and it was built on a corner, which would give her all the garden she needed. She was looking forward to creating a vegetable plot.

Sheila placed the brochure down on the coffee table. "Well, I know we haven't been back very long, but I agree that this cruise around the Mediterranean sounds very good."

"And we get to visit Venice again."

"Yes, but it's tinged with sadness as well as joy. It wasn't long after we got back the last time that Graham fell ill, and within three months, he was gone."

Gill gave Sheila a gentle hug. She wasn't given to demonstrative gestures but on this occasion, it was justified. "Now then, we've both done our mourning, and like you, I get things that remind me of the man I loved and lost, but we can't bring them back. We must embrace the memories and share our adventures with them in mind."

Sheila smiled. "You're right. We should book this cruise now."

They went over the itinerary, then Sheila rang the booking line. Both ladies sat waiting, listening to a monotonous voice telling them how important their call was as they waited for someone to respond.

Finally, the cruise consultant came online, and they started the booking arrangement. After asking and answering a few questions during the conversation with the advisor, it soon came to the deposit to secure the booking. Sheila looked at Gill, raised an eyebrow, and after getting a nod, she gave the necessary numbers to her account and the deposit was paid.

Now, with the cruise booked and the deposit paid, she closed the line and sat back.

"A drink of wine I think." Gill got up from the couch and walked to the kitchen. She had an open bottle and selected two large red wine glasses. She poured the remnants of the wine into the glasses and left the empty bottle on the counter before returning to her friend. "Cheers."

They clinked glasses and then each sipped and savoured the wine.

Sheila relaxed back into her seat. "I was just thinking about our last cruise and Martina. I wonder how she is now."

Gill placed her glass down carefully, steepled her fingers, and brought them to her lips, almost in the form of praying. Sheila knew that meant her friend was thinking deeply about the question.

After a few moments, she dropped her hands and picked up her wine glass. "You know, I did say we'd keep in touch, and we did swap emails, but I did nothing about it once we returned. It's very remiss of me, so as you've reminded me, I'll message her later on after you have gone."

"Is that a 'drink up and go' un-subtle hint?"

"I wouldn't quite put it like that, but dear friend, you've stacked an element of guilt on my shoulders, and I'd like to remove it before I forget what it was. But stay and relax, drink your wine, and don't worry about it."

Sheila held up her empty glass. "Clearly I'm not going to get a refill, so I may as well make my way home."

Gill smiled and stood as Sheila placed the glass on the table. "I may have an answer for you at the tea dance on Friday. Let me get your coat as you've decided to go."

Sheila followed Gill into the lobby, where she holding the coat open for her to slip her arms into. "You know, sometimes I question this friendship we have. The occasional dismissal, the parsimonious amount of wine on offer… Not to mention the way you always offer me as a partner to poor old Arthur Walters when he asks either one of us to dance with him on Friday's tea dance. Have you ever accepted a dance with him?"

"With my bad leg? No, never. I must say I do enjoy watching you walk around with him doing the quickstep."

"Hm. Funny how that bad leg gets so much better when Tony Sheppard comes over, and don't give me that, 'when you get to my age,' because that won't wash."

Gill clenched her fist and thrust it down as she responded.

"Curses! Found out again!"

The friends gave each other a light hug, then Sheila turned and opened the door. "I'll see you on Friday, and all I can hope is that your poor leg will be recovered enough to shock poor Arthur when you accept his offer of a dance."

"Take care, Sheila. I'll see you on Friday."

Gill watched Sheila walk down the path and go through the gate. She turned to give a brief wave then disappeared behind the hedge bordering the property as she went to her car. Gill closed the door and went into the dining area, where her computer was set up. She woke it up from the search they'd done about the cruise and opened her email account.

Now, how do I go about this message to Martina?

CHAPTER NINE

May

It was Friday when the two ladies next met up. Sheila had picked up Gill as usual and then drove down to Spillwell Village Hall for the afternoon tea dance. After they'd parked and were walking towards the hall, both ladies remembered when the call went out to save the hall.

The roof had let rain in over the years, but when the bridge club met for their usual weekly game, the sight that had greeted them was frightening. The middle two beams had fallen onto the dance floor, and rain had left a small lake in the building. The insurance company wouldn't pay out, stating that the building had not been kept in good repair. Most couldn't argue with that, but what to do?

Gill and Sheila set up a page on Facebook asking for donations and asked for people to help freely, people who could come and help rebuild the hall. Several builders said they would come on the weekend, and Sheila posted their company name, saying what a good company they were to give help to the community freely, and thus more offers came in.

The inside of the hall was cleared, and new beams spanning the hall were fitted, then Felicity Henshaw, a friend of Gill's from her girls' school days, contacted the committee and said she would donate £5,000 towards the rebuild. Others went to nearby towns, did fundraising, and advertised the things the new village hall would offer in the future.

Things just grew as the ladies and one man on the committee welcomed several new enquiries for the hall's use. Still with a flat roof but now with a slope from one side to the other and with better drainage, the village hall looked almost new.

The afternoon tea dance was getting quite busy as they paid the entrance fee and went into the community centre's hall. Marjory Sandhurst and Beryl Vester were already at their usual table. Gill and Sheila took their seats in what had become known as a single's corner.

The usual platitudes were exchanged and then they settled to wait for everyone else to come in and get seated.

Beryl leaned forward and pointed to a lady across the room who had just entered. "I don't know if you know her, but that poor woman went on a cruise recently. When she got back, she found she'd been burgled."

The woman was Tracy McCall, and the ladies knew her from serving tea at the interval.

Beryl then went on, "Not just the money, jewellery, and the like, but they removed furniture and emptied her garage of the wine she had in there. She said they were quite tidy, but whoever heard of tidy burglars? The police told her they've been getting a lot of these sort of absentee break-ins, but she still hasn't got over it."

Sheila looked at Gill then turned to Beryl. "Where does she live?"

"Kings Barton, just outside Winchester. She has one of those recent new builds that are springing up all over the place."

"You said she was burgled while she was on a cruise," Gill said. "Any idea when this happened and what boat she was on?"

"I think it was about two months ago, sometime in March. Ann Watson would know; she was the person who told me about it. Still, I suppose you could say some good came out of it. The man she's with came to her rescue and repaired the back door that the villains cut the hinges off to remove. They aren't a pair but both like dancing, so I suppose one could say, it has been a plus to a bad job."

Gill caught Sheila's eye and raised an eyebrow. Her friend wanted to have a quiet word, and most likely as soon as possible.

"You seem to be asking a lot of questions," Beryl said. "Has something like this happened to you?"

"No, not to us, but to a lady we got to know as we were cruising. The burglars broke into her house while she was with us."

"Did she live near here?"

"On the outskirts of Southampton, about a mile away on the Andover side."

"It's getting bad when they break into your house while you're away," Beryl said. "They could break into my house while I'm out shopping or while I'm here. They seem to know when we're out, don't they?"

"Yes, that's the puzzling thing about this, Beryl. It doesn't make sense to think they would park outside a house and watch people in the hope that they come out with a suitcase and get into a taxi." Sheila paused. "No, it's got to be simpler than that."

An announcement interrupted their thoughts as the host for the afternoon dance told them the new dance she would be demonstrating later. They listened, and shortly after, the first dance started. Tony Sheppard asked Beryl for the first dance. Arthur Walters came towards the group of ladies but asked Barbara Pullen if she would like the first waltz.

As they watched the two go onto the dance floor, Gill turned to Sheila. "This is strange, but when I messaged Martina, she messaged me back and asked if she could talk to me. Within a few minutes, she was telling me that a friend of hers had also had a break-in but very little was taken. Most had been put in storage because she was about to move."

"Another sea cruise victim?"

"No. That's the strange part about it. It was a river cruise and the break-in happened while she was away. She flew out to Germany and boarded the river boat there. She was robbed a few days later."

"Well, this breaks the pattern, but why?"

"That's the big question, Sheila, and I have no idea how to answer it."

"How about having a chat with Tracy during our tea break rather than speaking to Ann Watson about it?"

Once again, Gill managed to dodge dancing with Arthur Walters and ended up with Sheila going for a quickstep that was barely a trot. Still, he did his best, and the music was nice.

Eventually, it came to the break, and both ladies and a few

more on the committee went into the kitchen to prepare the tea and coffee. Once it was ready, they went to the counter and started tending to the recipients who'd formed two lines, one for coffee and the other for tea.

As Tracy McCall came to the front, Sheila leaned forward. "Tracy, can I have a quiet word a little later on—not about trying to get you on the committee, but about your break-in. Someone we know had the same thing happen to them, and we'd like to compare notes with you on how the police reacted to it."

"How did you get to hear about it, it didn't even get in the local newspaper?" Tracy asked.

"We were talking about the rotten luck our friend had, and Beryl Vester said you'd had the same bad luck, so I thought it would be good to have a few words to see if the way it was done was the same. The police seem to think it's a random thing, but Gill and I don't."

"How about I meet you after the dance outside, and you can ask your questions and also tell me if it sounds the same? Goodness, you sound like those women in a book I read a short while ago… Something about a murder club, but this is nothing like that."

Once the tea break was over, the dancing resumed and once again, Gill dodged Arthur Walters' offer of a dance, so Sheila was walked around the floor for a waltz that sometimes almost managed to be in time to the music. She thanked Arthur for the dance, then glared at Gill, who rubbed her knee as if in answer to the unspoken question.

The dance ended, and the committee members started to tidy up as the rest of the members put on their coats and left them to it. Once all was cleared, and as the centre was waiting to be locked up, Sheila and Gill stepped out from the hall and saw Tracy McCall waiting for them by her car.

They said goodbye to Carol, who was locking the door, and joined Tracy.

"Let's sit in the car," said Tracy, and she opened the back door for the ladies. Once inside, Tracy got in the front driver's seat and turned to face them. "Okay. You have my attention. What do you want to know?"

"First, let me explain our interest. While we were on a cruise, a single lady had her house broken into it and a lot of things were stolen. Some were large items, and lots were small but valuable. The police felt it was a well-organised gang but couldn't see how the fact that she was on a cruise had any link to the burglary. So, the first question is, did your break-in occur while you were on a cruise? We were told that it had, but just to be sure, is that true?"

"Yes, it did. I wasn't informed by anyone, though. I just unlocked the front door and saw the burglar alarm wasn't on. The case had some sort of foam all over it. Then I noticed the umbrella stand that should be in the hall was missing, and I knew I'd been robbed."

"So how did they get in?" asked Gill.

"The police found that they had gone around the back of the house and cut one pane of glass out of the kitchen window. Then they must've crawled in and opened the front door."

"Was other furniture or any special artefacts taken?"

"Yes, how did you know?" Tracey asked.

"Because the lady we were with had furniture removed, and her son hadn't missed it when he did a rough inventory of things he knew his mother had. They'd also opened her safe and taken her father's medals from the last war and her grandfathers, along with a lot of other high value items."

"I don't have a safe," said Tracy. "Not enough to my name to warrant one. When Paul, my husband died, we'd already liquidised most of our savings in stocks and shares to try to get help for him. The cancer was very quick, and he was gone in under two months. It's a hell of a way to go. I watched helplessly as he shrank down to skin and bones, but he never stopped smiling at me when I came into the bedroom."

"We're so sorry, Tracy but thank you for helping us with this. Did the burglars take much?"

"We had a Victorian musical box that Paul bought me for a wedding anniversary." She paused and took a deep breath. "Sorry, it still catches me. It was a lovely memory, and now it's gone. They took lots of silly things like the coffee-making machine. It wasn't worth a lot, but they also emptied the cupboards and cleared all the sachets of coffee for it. We had a small folding table, and they took that… Paul's leather coat, they took that, and worst of all, all his cigarette cards mounted in books. All our wine and spirits were stolen, and all our silver or gold too. My mother's silver tea set was part of that, and a few of my necklaces that were worth something. They took the TV from the wall mounting, and my laptop and iPad I had for playing silly games on. The strange thing was, they were very tidy. I've known other people who have been burgled before this, and they found their drawers' dumped all over the floor. These people seemed to have lifted everything out, then very carefully put things back in the same drawer. It was all very strange."

"Yes," said Gill. "Martina said the same thing. It adds to the puzzle, doesn't it? It's as if they're being respectful about robbing you! I haven't been able to tell Sheila yet, but Martina has told me that she knows of another break-in while they f were on a cruise. She told the police, but they say they can't see the significance of the cruise to the break-in, other than they weren't at home." Gill paused, wondering about the connection. "Tracy, did you talk to anyone on the cruise ship or mention your address to them?"

"No, I'm sure I didn't." She looked up at the roof of her car as if recalling something. "Well, other than when I went to the future bookings' desk. But I only confirmed my postcode and the first line of my address. They had it already, so it was merely a security check."

"Was anyone nearby who could've overheard you?" Sheila asked.

"No. People came and picked up leaflets from a desk near my seat, but no one stayed to overhear my answers."

"Oh, well. That kills that idea," said Sheila. "It just needed someone to be waiting to see the future cruise agent, and we might have got a lead, since the police aren't interested."

Tracy was quiet for a moment, her brow furrowed. "There *is* one thing I just remembered. One of the dance hosts was waiting to speak to her, but he's part of the ship's staff. He'd told me he would be going down to see her to find out what further cruises he might be joining. Gerald Portman is a wonderful dancer and so polite, and he was most sympathetic when I told him how my husband died."

"But he could have overheard you talking to the agent?"

"Well, yes. He was nearby, but he was filling in a form and placed it into a basket by the future tour's representative before he excused himself and went away."

"Was this after you'd confirmed your postcode and the first line of your address?"

"Well, I suppose it might have been. We were searching for availability at that point."

There was silence in the car as the ladies mulled over this new information. The sound of sudden rain on the car roof broke the silence.

"Thank you, Tracy," Gill said. "It's still not conclusive, but just maybe, the dance host is a link. Sheila and I have met him too. He danced with both of us and with Martina. But she didn't book another cruise on board, so that puts a doubt on that being a possible way forward."

"Just another thought, Tracy. We know you live near here, but how near?"

"I live in Flexford, just outside of Ampfield. I''s handy for Plymouth and Southampton, and it's one of the new areas that are springing up all over the place."

"Thanks, Tracy, and I guess the police haven't linked the cruise ship to the theft."

"Well, no. They thought it was just a random break-in."

They sat in silence for four or five minutes. "The rain has stopped," Sheila said. "I think it's time to say goodbye to you, Tracy, and we'd better be on our way."

They both got out of the car, waved to Tracy as she drove away, and walked to Sheila's car, avoiding the puddles as they went.

Once comfortably seated in the car and buckled up, Gill said, "The dance host link is a bit tenuous, but with so many burglaries in the Southampton area, I do wonder if the nice guy who danced with us is in fact not a nice guy at all."

As Sheila drove away from the village hall, the rain started once again. She put her lights on because it was so dark it was almost as if night-time had come early. They were late, and traffic had begun to build up, and it was close to the time for the school run.

"I wonder if they are operating all along the south coast," Gill said. "Cruise ships go from Dover and occasionally from London. If it's a London gang, that would suit them perfectly."

"You would've made a good detective, Gill." Sheila made a left turn to continue on their way.

"You think so? It must be my analytical mind that's inspiring me."

"No, I don't think it's that. It's the way you can work out courses of action. For instance, how you once again managed to dodge out of dancing with Arthur Walters. That takes a cunning mind. Maybe I should rephrase my observation. Maybe it should be that you would have made a clever crook. With your ducking and weaving, you'd never get caught."

They both laughed and Sheila said, "Might be worth checking to see if anyone further along the coast towards London has also been on a cruise and been robbed."

"How would we do that?"

"Social media," said Sheila.

"Well, don't count on me for that. I don't twit, that's for birds, or put my face in any book, and tick tock is for grandfather clocks, so count me out on that too. Why people can't just phone one another and talk? I don't understand it."

"How did you contact Martina?" Sheila asked with a smile.

Gill looked at Sheila, who kept her eyes on the road.

"Well, I used email, as you know, but that was because she asked me to keep in touch that way. I'd prefer to talk to someone rather than this text messaging young people do."

Sheila slowed the car and turned into Gill's street. The rain still poured down and as she stopped outside Gill's house, thunder and lightning cracked the sky, and the rain intensified.

They both lived in Spillwell, near Ampfield between Winchester and Southampton. Sheila, having sold her house after her husband died, saw the new buildings still being constructed and decided she would move away from her marital home to create new memories. Her house was a few streets away from Gill's.

Sheila turned off the car's engine, and they sat listening to the rain pounding down onto the car roof and bonnet.

"So, this is the result of global warming," Gill said and tutted. "We get monsoon storms in dear old England."

"Looking at the water running down the road, if it keeps falling like this—" A flash of lightning followed closely by the rumble of thunder interrupted her. "—we might find out if this car can float."

The rain continued to lash down, then suddenly slowed and almost stopped.

"That's me," said Gill and opened the car door. "I'll leave you to try your media thingy, and I'll have you know, my knee *is* giving me quite a bit of pain now."

Sheila smiled. "Don't worry, dear, Arthur Walters won't be asking you to dance for another fortnight, so it has plenty of time to get better."

Gill wrinkled her nose. "I just hope so. I do get so much pain with my bad leg. Speak to you later." And she walked up the path to her front door with a pronounced limp.

After Gill had gone into her house, Sheila continued to her own house. Once she settled indoors, she decided to send out a query about any others who'd had thefts whilst on a cruise or after having had one. It was a long shot, but there was something very odd indeed about all these strangely tidy burglaries.

CHAPTER NINE

July

The long-awaited visit to the Jamieson house arrived and having checked the departure, a few nights later, the plan came into action.

They made it into the field, parked next to the fence, and used the battery handsaw to cut the ties and remove a section of fence. Getting into the house hadn't been such a problem from the rear; they removed a pane of glass, and once Billy was inside, he soon immobilised the alarm system.

They'd all gone through the house, bagging anything that caught their eye. Robert watched, checking that special items were bubble-wrapped and directing them to the heavier items. The TV, once disconnected from the wall, was wrapped up and taken out. This one was a top-of-the-range set. Robert made sure to pocket the controller too.

The silver-framed pictures with the grandchildren went—she could always get other prints—and the four-matching vases were a very nice find. The Hornby double-O boxed train sets and their few accessories were bundled up, along with three fur coats, pearls, and gold and silver necklaces found in a jewellery box in the bedroom.

Max, one of the helpers who took over if anyone couldn't do their shift and on this occasion had taken over from John, found a bundle of old comics in a suitcase under the bed. He also found a suitcase of old postcards from the First World War and some after. What looked like a quality Turkish rug was removed, as well as an old rocking chair. They took the quality wine cabinet, and the bottles were placed in wine boxes for safety. The malt whisky might find its way into Robert's office for personal attention!

The cellar provided more cases of wine and spirits. Wooden boxes were pressed into use, and they soon emptied the racks. They took an old rocking horse and a doll's house with all the bits and bobs in it up the steps from the cellar and loaded in onto the lorry. Leaning against the wall and covered with sacking was a broken frame with a painting of a horse. No one thought it would have any great value, but they removed it anyway. If in doubt, take it out.

But the best thing they found was a writing desk in a locked room, and after moving it into the lorry, they found a door that opened to reveal a large safe. Robert remembered the green book he'd flipped through in a drawer in the desk and had run out to the lorry. He opened the drawer, took out the green book and returned to the safe. There in the book was the safe code number. Billy turned the dials as Robert called the numbers, and the safe opened.

Stacks of money were inside, along with cases full of necklaces, bracelets, and even a tiara. They put everything into a large bag, most things with cases, but some in presentation boxes. Robert had drooled over the medals but had almost choked when a box was opened which contained gold South African Krugerrands. They were each in an individual little plastic sleeve, all eighty-one of them shouting money to his ears. Robert almost left a thank you note to her for leaving the green book.

There were a few other items in the safe, and Priceright took everything. They were on their way back to base after a two-hour visit, feeling very pleased with themselves indeed.

***

Partner had taken a break from his cruising and met up with Robert to go over the details of the assets they had and the projected values they could expect.

The list was quite long, and Partner, who was reading Tracy McCall's removal, had said that the silver tea set being melted down for the value to be worthwhile. The cigarette cards would attract interest, as would the Victorian musical box, but the rest would be only a small amount for the pot.

As Partner sat reading the list, Robert said, "I want your opinion on a painting we found in the cellar of the Jamieson's house. We lifted it, but it had a broken frame. It's a painting of a horse. It looks quite good, but why would she want to have her horse painted?"

"Where is it, Robert?"

"It's in the lockup. I wouldn't keep it here."

"Let's take a look then." Partner pulled his jacket on. He looked out of the window to check if it was raining, then left his topcoat and started down the stairs to the working area.

Robert followed and after closing the main door, got into Partner's runabout car. They drove to the lockup, and once they'd checked no one was around, opened it.

The damaged painting was near the door, and as Partner unwrapped it, he gasped. "I think this is a Stubbs painting."

"Worth anything?"

Partner looked at Robert in amazement. "Have you not heard of George Stubbs? He was a master of painting horses. His paintings have been sold for twenty to forty million each."

Priceright almost fell over as blood drained from his head, and he turned white with shock. "For a picture of a black horse? This Stubbs guy didn't even paint the background very well. What's the world coming to if that's supposed to be great art?"

"We need to check if it's genuine first. Then we'll get the frame repaired and get it valued. I'll get in touch with my Arab friend and let him know that we may have a very valuable painting that he might be interested in. Do you know anyone who's into paintings by a master that could authenticate it and could do with a little extra cash?"

"No. Not my sort of thing. How about we wait? And when the insurance claim goes in, we try to find out what's on the list being claimed?"

"Well, that's not a bad idea." Partner brushed a speck of dust from his jacket. "Who do you know on the crime squad?"

"I know a man who knows a copper."

"Makes the chain too long. Leave it with me. I'll talk to an acquaintance I know who works in Christie's. The police may get in touch with them to warn them of a stolen piece of art."

Partner took out his phone and snapped a few shots of the

painting. "Leave it like that for now, unrepaired, and wrap it up well, in case it does turn out to be an original. Oh, and put it up on top of something flat and high in case this place gets flooded."

"Right, Partner. I'm glad I thought to bring it. A painting of a horse, whatever next?"

"Let's get back to your place, and we can go over the list of the rest of the stuff."

They left the lockup and returned to the storeroom and Robert's quarters upstairs.

Once comfortable again, Partner read through the list and the estimated values once again. When he was finished, he placed the list down on the table and stood.

"Well, Robert, I must be going. Lots to do before my next voyage. I'm going to talk to a lady I know about a horse."

"Be careful. We don't want this little set-up blown now."

"She knows I work on behalf of a few Arab buyers. In fact, I bid for a Roman vase for one of them a short while ago. I'll see what's in the wind." He stood and pulled on his topcoat. "The McCall items look good. The umbrella stand and Victorian musical box aren't high-priced items, but they all add up. The cigarette cards in a book will give a good return—they're always well-sought-after items. Yes, overall, a good haul. Well done."

***

A tall well-dressed man walked into the foyer of Christie's and approached the reception desk.

"Hello again, Mr. Portman," the receptionist said and gave him a beaming smile. "Miss Prescott asked me to buzz you through. She's waiting for you."

"Thank you, Marianne. Please tell her I'm on my way up." He pushed the call button on the lift and the doors opened. He entered and pressed for floor two. When he exited, he saw Helen waiting at her office door.

When he reached out to take hold of her shoulders and kiss her cheek, she stepped back and offered her hand. A little bit perplexed, he shook her hand. Helen stepped back and waved him into her room.

She closed the door and sat behind her desk. "Potential business or actual?"

"My goodness, Helen. No 'how are you? You're looking good.' Just straight to business."

"Those days are long past, Mr. Portman. It's business from now on, and I don't mean hanky-panky business."

"Helen, I'd really like to get past all this hostility. As I explained once before, if I were ever to consider marriage, then you would be my ideal partner. I just can't think about that part of my life yet. At least call me by my first name while I quiz your expert knowledge on a possible painting one of my Arab clients has been offered."

She softened a little and sat forward. "Okay then, Gerald, to business. What's the painting?"

He showed her the photos on his phone. "This is the photo my client sent me. He's worried that it's stolen or not an original."

"Really? Well, let me look at it."

He handed her the phone, and she looked at it, then smiled. "This looks like a Stubbs painting, but I have my doubts."

"Oh, and why would that be?"

"Let me send this to my email account here, then I can blow it up on the screen projector."

She fiddled with his phone and then passed it back to Gerald. As she waited for the photo to arrive, she studied the man opposite. He had wined and dined her over several months, and they had eventually both gone back to her flat in Kensington. He was an attentive lover, she had to admit that, but when it came to the word love, he made it very clear that wasn't for him.

Her machine pinged and she opened the photo. She moved to the big screen that slowly dropped down the wall. Once it stopped, she pointed a small control unit at her computer and the photo came up on the screen.

Gerald got up and moved nearer to her, looking at the huge projection on the screen.

"Well, it's not an original. It looks like a fairly good copy, and there are lots of artists out there who can do a quite good job of it, but this is just that: a copy. You should tell your Arab client not to buy it."

"How can you be so sure, Helen?"

"Because this is supposed to be a George Stubbs painting of Lord Grosvenor's horse called Sweet William in a landscape, but as Christie's sold this… Hold on a moment," she said and went back to her computer. She tapped a few keys. "Yes, here it is. It was sold on 20th November 1987, lot number twenty-six. An anonymous sale to a private collection. It has since been sold by Sotheby's on July 4th, 2019. They have provided no further information, so one must assume that like us, it was an anonymous sale and another private purchaser."

Gerald stepped back, still staring at the screen. He felt gutted.

"You look as if you've already purchased it and now you know you have a dud on your hands."

Gerald shook his head. "No, Helen. I'm so glad that you were able to help me on this. Now I need to contact my client and break the bad news to him."

They returned to the desk as Helen turned the projector off and it rolled up again.

He sat down opposite Helen who sat and swivelled her chair around to look at him. "Tell me, Gerald, with all your knowledge of paintings, although you're not in my class, did you really expect this," she pointed to the screen, "to be genuine?"

"No, but there's always a chance, and the bonus was I got to see you again."

"Oh, no, mister. You can turn your charm mode off. You and I are now just business contacts: me on one side of the fence, you on the other. Would you like me to continue to message you if any genuine paintings come up for auction or shall I delete your email address as a waste of time?"

"Oh, that's hurtful, Helen. Yes, please keep me informed. And may I see you again sometime in the next few weeks, possibly for lunch, just to say thank you on behalf of my client?"

"I don't think that's going to happen, do you? I will get

Marianne to send my bill to you, and as I'm in a good mood, I'll only charge you for one hour of my time. That's a saving of a quarter of an hour at my chargeable rate. You should get it tomorrow by email."

"But, Helen, we're friends. Surely this was just a conversation between friends?"

"Business, remember. I've recorded our conversation, so unless you shift your backside out of that chair, I might need to increase my fee for time-wasting. Good day, Mr. Portman." She rose and walked to the door to open it, standing aside as he walked through, looking quite dejected. As he turned to say something more, she stepped back. "You know your way out." And she shut the door.

He stood for a moment looking at the closed door, then turned and walked to the lift.

As he exited the lift, he glanced at Marianne and thought she had a smirk on her face. Could she have listened in on the conversation?

He left the building and stopped outside on the pavement. He turned and looked up at the second-floor window he thought was Helen's, then shook his head in disbelief and walked away.

He hadn't been looking up at the correct window, but Helen *had* watched him on the pavement below. She sighed and returned to her chair. She recalled their last bedroom conversation. She had brought up the subject of marriage, but he had told her that he had a different M word, and he didn't want to change the very nice arrangement they had.

She had been lying in his arms but she'd sat up. "What arrangement?"

"This. The casual meetings now and then, and the lovemaking. I'll be faithful to you, as you are to me, but marriage, no. Mistress, yes."

She had got out of bed and told him to get out and take all his bits with him. This mistress had had enough. He had remonstrated with her, but she had picked up one of his shoes and threw it at his chest.

"Make sure you're gone by the time I get out of the shower," she had said as she left him getting dressed.

She shook her head. *Thank goodness I didn't give that asshole a key to my apartment.*

***

Robert sat at his desk going over the bookings for his limo service and the removal business. With all the vehicles out on jobs, the place was empty. He heard someone slam the single door at the end of the building shut. He started to get up from his chair when a voice came echoing up from the warehouse below.

"Robert, I'm coming up to see you. Sorry to wake you."

Oh great. Partner in a foul mood. Just what I wanted when I was ending my day on a high.

Partner stomped in without knocking and looked at Robert who leaned on his desk, looking at a rather drunk Partner. Shaking his head and staggering a little, he pulled his topcoat off and sat down in one of the easy chairs, dropping his coat on the floor.

"Well, this is an unexpected delight. What's caused you to drop in and interrupt my evening work on the accounts."

"I know, Robert, but I'm just about up to here," he put a flat hand up to his forehead, "with women."

"Bit pissed off then, are we?"

"That just about sums it up." He leaned forward and said, "I went to see my friend Helen in Christie's earlier today, and she bombed me off. I spent ages cultivating our relationship, but she took the hump after our last interlude in bed."

Robert moved over to the other armchair and sat down opposite him. As Partner started imparting this juicy bit of conversation, his attention was totally on what his next sentence would be.

"Oh, I thought you were coming over to offer me a stiff drink, not to get comfortable. Give me a shot of that fine malt whisky you have. I will say one thing about you, Robert, you do appreciate the quality of a good whisky."

Groaning, Robert went to his cabinet and took the bottle out. He picked up two glasses and placed them on a small table in front of both seats. After pouring a measure into each glass, he put the bottle down, then passed one glass to his partner. He took his own glass and returned to his chair.

Partner was looking at the glass of whisky, shaking his head. "You know, Robert, I thought Helen and I were a good pair. I would ring her whenever I was in town, and she would ring or message me if she had a need to celebrate after a particular auction had gone through. She was particularly demanding after she had totalled up the sales commission and calculated what her percentage would be. Funny how percentages can turn a girl on." Partner lifted the glass and tossed the contents down. He took the bottle and poured another measure.

Robert grimaced as he looked at the remnants moving around the bottle as Partner placed it back on the table. He hadn't even lifted his glass to his lips yet.

"I never moaned if she said we couldn't meet up the weekend I was in London, and she likewise never moaned when I told her I was working abroad. It was an amicable arrangement and worked for us both."

Robert nodded as Partner lifted his glass and took a large mouthful, leaving a very small amount in his glass as he placed it on the table. Robert took a sip from his glass, and let it roll around before swallowing it down, appreciating the sensations that burst on his taste buds.

"We were in her bed after a very satisfying time together when she asked a question that somehow my answer upset her," Partner said, his voice quite slurred.

Robert lifted his glass and took another sip, waiting for the nitty-gritty.

Partner reached for the whisky bottle, poured in a larger measure, and then placed the bottle back onto the table. Looking at the bottle, Robert gave up on any likelihood of any remaining for another day.

As Robert was looking at the bottle, his partner lifted the recharged glass and continued, "Cheers, Robert, you're a good listener to a friend in need." He drank a good slug, then placed the glass down on the table. "Where was I? Oh, yes, bloody Helen."

Definitely pissed off and getting more so at the expense of my whisky.

Partner sighed and emptied the glass. He took the bottle, emptied the remains into his glass, and placed the empty bottle back on the table.

Robert savoured another sip as it slipped down, whilst looking at the bottle like a dead friend. "What caused you all this distress?"

"Love. The bloody L word came up. She started talking about us making our arrangement more permanent, and we should maybe talk about marriage. I said I liked the arrangement as it was, and that our situation starts with an M, so why change it?"

Robert sat back. M? what the hell was he was talking about? Then it hit him. "Mistress. You wanted her as a mistress?"

"Well, yes. We'd been very comfortable up to then, but when she realised that I was referring to her as my mistress and had no intention of getting married, she went berserk. She got out of bed and started throwing my clothes at me, shouting for me to get out of her place. Then she threw my shoes at me and told me to be out of her apartment by the time she came from her shower or she'd call security. Robert, she looked wonderful as she went naked into the bathroom and slammed the door."

"Well, why don't you marry the girl? The state you're in, you clearly do love her."

"Heaven's above, don't you start saying that to me. It's the last thing I want."

"Okay. Let's forget all that. Did she answer the question on the horse painting?"

"Oh, yes. She took great delight in informing me that it was just a copy of the original. That's most likely why it was broken and left in the cellar."

"So, no value at all."

"A small amount, but it might be better to burn it. No trace then back to us," said Partner.

"There go my retirement plans." Robert drank the last of his malt and stood. He picked up the empty bottle, walked over to the sink and placed the glass and bottle down on the side. As he returned, he noticed Partner had finished his whisky and was slumped down in the chair and. He was clearly not able to drive home.

Robert went to the sofa, lifted the seat, and pulled out the bed from inside the base. He made the bed up and then returned to his partner.

"Come on, Gerald, you're staying over with me tonight." Robert helped him to the prepared bed and pulled his shoes off, then as the drink took hold even more, he pulled his arms from the jacket he was wearing, getting no resistance or help. Partner collapsed backwards onto the bed, and Robert pulled his partner's trousers off. He lifted his feet, turned him onto the bed, then pulled the sheet and bed covers over him.

He looked down at Partner, now totally out of it, sleeping with most of Robert's bottle of good malt whisky in him. Shaking his head, Robert turned the light off and went into his bedroom. *What a turn-up for the books. Partner in love, and the chance of a big return on a horse painting galloping off.*

CHAPTER TEN

July

There was a light breeze and the sun shone down through wispy clouds when the ladies met at the park gates.

Sheila and Gill met up for their usual eleven o'clock stroll around the lake. Today's stroll was to be slightly different; they had to talk about the messages and replies that Shelia had received. They also had one other person with them: Martina.

As they walked, they listened to Sheila telling them of the replies she'd had from her request for people who had been robbed while on or after a cruise. There were many, and all were from along the South coast.

She had asked for a surname and a district in a county, and the response was far more than she had expected. The cases stretched from Dover all along the coast to one case in Dartmouth, quite a few were around London, and then the next concentrated amount was around and near Southampton. The lady in Dartmouth was the earliest, being three years ago. Martina was one of the latest.

Coming to a bench, the ladies sat. Sheila took out a few sheets of paper and showed the two ladies the list, and then showed them a sheet with a map of the south coast from Dover to Dartmouth with little red dots on it. "This map correlates to the list. In each case, I have divided the counties and marked roughly where the theft was. In our area, the furthest north seems to be Kingsworthy, just north of Winchester and in striking distance of Southampton. And around London, it seems to be Rickmansworth, just to the north-west of London. Again, Dover becomes the nearest port to it, but in all cases, both Southampton, Portsmouth, and Dover aren't a great barrier for travelling from the southern counties."

The two ladies looked at the list, then the map, and then again to the list.

"Sheila, I can't believe you had such a huge response.

It's amazing, and you've added the extra one I found out about," said Martina. "Thirty-seven cases. Is there no end to the misery these people are causing?"

"There's no doubt that they're on a run, but we now have something to show the police," said Gill.

"It won't get my stuff back," said Martina, "but I would love to see these people put behind bars."

"Then if you're in agreement, why don't we go to the central police station in Southampton and show them what evidence we have here, and see if they start an investigation," suggested Gill.

"That, I'm afraid, is going to be down to both of you. As you know, the burglary has totally unnerved me, and I'm only a week away from moving. So, ladies, my good friends, I need to say goodbye, but hope that you will, once I'm settled in, come, and visit me. I would love to keep in touch."

"We'll contact the police tomorrow to make an appointment," Gill said as she stood, "but for now, let's just wander around the park and enjoy ourselves."

They passed the paperwork to Sheila and then started walking again, each with their own thoughts on the subject they had been discussing, and in their own way enjoying their company and the warm July sunshine.

***

Robert woke early and came from his bedroom to find Gerald holding his head and groaning. Robert smiled as he noted the bloodshot eyes and haggard face that regarded his entrance. "Well," he said, "you really tied one on last night. You'd better marry that girl; you've got it bad."

"Can you talk a little softer? I think you must have hit me with something. My head's throbbing as if it's been clubbed."

"No, Partner, your pain is all self-inflicted. You climbed into my bottle of whisky and tried embalming from the inside out." Robert turned to the kitchen section and filled the kettle and set it to boil. Once that was done, he took out a frying pan, making quite a lot of noise in doing so, and said, "Fancy a nice bacon sandwich for breakfast?"

Partner just looked at him, still holding his head.

"I'll take that as a no then," he said as he turned the heat on under the pan and then went to the fridge to get the bacon.

The kettle started to whistle as it boiled, and he turned it off after he glanced at Partner and saw the agony on his face. Most satisfying, he thought. With the bacon pack in his hand, he pushed the fridge door closed with a satisfactory thud and grinned as he watched the result it had on his hungover partner.

He stripped the first piece of bacon out from the pack and held it up for Partner to see. "It's nice and lean, should you change your mind." He dropped the first piece into the pan and grinned as it began to give a lovely sizzling sound as it cooked. The sizzling increased as three more strips joined the first.

Partner stood, none too steady on his feet, glared at Robert, then made a dash to the toilet with his hand over his mouth,

That will teach you not to drink all my whisky. He busied himself making his tea and bacon sarnies, then left the kitchen after making sure all the heating was off. Partner was just coming from the bathroom as Robert made his way to the lounge and put the TV on.

Partner returned to the sofa bed and lay back down on it.

The weather forecast started as the TV tuned in, and Robert nudged the sound up a few more points to make sure Partner got the full benefit.

"You're a nasty bugger, Robert. Turn the bloody thing off and let me die in peace."

"Oh, sorry, Gerald, I forgot. It's not often I get to have a person stay overnight these days. Now what did I do with that controller?" He let the TV programme stay on a little longer, before finding the remote controller that he had by his side.

Once the TV was off, he continued with his bacon sandwich, aware that the smell, as it always did, starting to drift around the room.

Again, Partner rose quickly from the bed and rushed to the bathroom, and Robert chomped on his breakfast as Partner emptied his stomach. It didn't alter Robert's enjoyment of his breakfast; it really was a delicious revenge.

Gerald staggard from the bathroom, sniffed, then turned and rushed back into the bathroom to regale Robert with some more distressing sounds that pleased him even further.

A few minutes passed, and then as Robert stood to take his empty plate to the kitchen, Partner, now a horrible grey colour, came from the bathroom.

"Feeling better now?" asked Robert in his best caring voice.

"Do you have an air spray? The bathroom stinks from my suffering, and it smells awful out here with your breakfast stench."

Robert tutted as he went into the bathroom, located the can, and gave it a good spray to dispel the acrid smell left by Gerald's discomfort. He returned to the living area, where Partner was sitting on the edge of the sofa bed, pulling his trousers on.

"I need to get home, Robert, but I'll need you to drive me. You can leave my car on the drive, and then take the Tube back here."

"Sorry, I have things to do. I'll ring for a taxi, and you can collect your car sometime in the future. I will drop it into the garage underneath here, and Badger can juggle the vehicles once he gets back. We have the auction in two days' time, and I'm going down with the next load to Bristol to make sure everything is up together."

"Okay, Robert, do that and I'll talk to you soon."

Robert rang for a taxi, and it arrived a few moments after Partner was dressed.

Gerald thanked Robert for his help with the overnight bed and slowly went down the wooden steps into the empty storage space for the removal vans. Gingerly he got into the taxi, gave the destination to the driver, and winced as Robert slammed the door shut on the taxi before waving goodbye.

Robert heard nothing from Partner until three days later when the auction was over, and he returned to collect his car.

"Well, you look much better." He greeted Gerald as he ticked his checklist and then told Andrew, the driver of the removal van, to let him know if there were any difficulties on the job. He watched Andrew drive from the bay, and once clear, he closed the doors, watching them drop down to enclose Partner's car in the bay. "We need to talk before you go. Come on upstairs."

"Do we have a problem?" asked Partner as he followed Robert upstairs.

"No, not in so many words, but I want to talk about the distribution of our wealth."

"Someone is creaming the top off our profits?"

"Sit down." Robert sat opposite Partner and then waded straight in. "I think we need to relook at the way the money is split up. A fairer sharing would be 40% to you, and 60% to me."

Gerald leaned forward. "What?"

Robert held up his hand. "I have all the costs and risks. I pay the lads from my share, and you take 50% with no deductions. I don't think that's a fair distribution of the money."

Partner sat back, shaking his head. "I don't believe what I'm hearing. This caper is my creation. I asked you to do it, thus, I employ you. You and those who help you are employed and paid by you from your half. Make no mistake about it: I call the shots, not you. Don't get greedy on me Robert because I can easily go elsewhere to get it done. The money is going up as we get more and more clients, and your 50% goes up also, but how you adjust the share you get to give your employees a bit more is none of my business, but it's not coming out of my percentage. Are we clear on this, Robert? Because if I dissolve this partnership now, and my 50% is not in my bank within the usual five days, a few Arab friends will call on you and convince you that the best thing to do is pay me my share plus the cost of their fee."

Robert looked quite shaken as he listened to Partner. He hadn't expected this reaction at all; it was like he was talking to a different person to the man he knew. Composing himself, Robert leaned forward. "Okay. For the moment, it stays as is, but as to me being employed, forget that. You offered a partnership at the outset of this caper, so there's no employment between you and me. Secondly, our relationship is now on a different basis. You don't threaten me and think I'm going to sit on my ass and live in fear." He lifted the phone he had been holding and took a photo of Partner.

"Hey. Why the photo of me? You know I don't allow any traceable elements in this deal. Wipe it off now."

Robert pressed a few buttons. "Just sent it to a friend of mine who will find you and terminate the enterprise permanently. Like I said, I don't like threats, and you threatened the wrong man in me."

"Look, Robert, I didn't say I would arrange that now. I reminded you that the arrangement was for 50% each, and you should make sure I got the percentage we agreed on at the start."

"Have I ever cheated you? You've always got your agreed share, but when I asked you about a better distribution, you changed into a wannabe gangster, threatening my life. Now, are we talking? Or are we going our own way? Only my assassin is one that will let you know why your accidental death is occurring before it happens—he's kind like that."

Gerald shook his head. "Robert, you live in a dark, dark place if you can arrange that. Okay, much against my better judgement, I'll take 40%, and you share the extra between the lads. After all, they do pick up a few things that you might miss."

"Dark place, no. Grey, yes. Now that we've agreed on this change, the auction we just had a few days ago will be divided fifty-fifty, and the new arrangement will start from there."

Partner stood and offered his hand. "To a new arrangement, and I hope the next auction brings an even bigger amount than the last. We must have a meeting soon to discuss the totals."

Robert took the offered hand and shook it, but the itch was now more like chicken pox, his whole body was quivering. All was not well.

Robert opened the warehouse door for Gerald to drive out.

As Partner got to the doorway where Robert stood, he stopped. "Don't forget to delete that photo, remember. No evidence means the law can't pin anything on us."

"I didn't take one. You see, I play harder than you. But I didn't lie about my friendly assassin; he very much does exist."

Partner drove away from the garage, and Robert looked at his phone. *I wish I had taken that photo.*

CHAPTER ELEVEN

July

Detective Inspector Wainwright looked at the stack of files on his desk and shook his head. *Either the villains have been working overtime, or I've been asleep on the neverending job.*

The desk he was sitting behind was stacked with yellow folders on one end, and one lonely yellow folder with a red line on it had been placed at the other end. His desk was tidy, his pens and notebooks laid out in a regular order, not that it was his doing. By his own admission, he was an untidy bugger, but Sandra, his helpful investigating officer, had cleared this ready for him to start work.

As he looked at the stack of folders waiting for his attention, the door opened and his lifesaver assistant came in with two cups of tea, one very milky, the other, so dark, it looked as if no milk had been added.

Sandra placed the dark brew in front of her boss and walked to the window to look down over the streets below. "Traffic's building up again. With two cruise ships in the port, the taxis are all in full swing. Nice day for it, though."

Wainwright grunted and leaned back into his groaning chair to swivel around to look at his assistant. "It's today you arranged for those two women to come and speak to me about a burglary, isn't it?"

"Yes, and it's not just about one burglary: it's about a lot. As I told you, they say they have compelling information that could help solve quite a few of our cases, all in one sweep. They wanted to come the day they rang, but I told them you were very busy, but you could manage an eleven o'clock appointment today."

Wainwright looked at the pile of folders. "Okay, I'll start wading through these and sorting them. You wheel them in when they arrive, but you'd better stay in here to take any notes in case they really do have something of interest." He placed the tea down on his table, and as he sat forward, the chair groaned once again. "You say they're mature ladies... Is that the euphemism for old ladies, or dare I say it, pensioners?"

"I think they're both retired, but both sounded as if they have all their marbles with them. Be nice to them, even if they do turn out to be just well-intentioned people."

"Heaven help me from good intentions, in any form. The public solving issues on our behalf can only lead to some sort of disaster."

"Drink your liquid tar. You'll feel better after that." Sandra smiled and left her boss to go through the folders. They had a good working arrangement, and neither took nor gave offence to their banter. It was now routinely accepted that she only addressed him as sir in the presence of a superior officer. It had been his instruction, and she was more than happy to go with it.

Almost an hour later when D.I. Wainwright got a call that his two visitors were on the way up to meet him for his eleven o'clock appointment. Two chairs had been brought into his office, and they sat in front of his now untidy desk. Pieces of paper with notes on them, attached with paper clips to the yellow folders, were scattered around his desk. The biggest pile was on the floor to one side.

Sandra knocked on the door and ushered in two ladies. They hardly fitted his mental description of pensioners, with both standing on their own two feet and no sight of a Zimmer or a wheelchair.

The inspector stood, and the chair gave a sound almost like a sigh as his bulk was removed from it.

The taller of the two stepped forward and put out her hand. "Thank you for agreeing to see us, inspector. May I do the introductions?" She turned and pointed to her colleague. "This is my very good friend Sheila Chancel, and my name is Gillian Blakeney. I prefer my name shortened to Gill, should you wish to be less formal during this discussion."

D.I. Wainwright shook hands with them both and asked them to sit down. *Certainly, all their marbles are intact.* He lowered himself into the protesting chair. "I'm afraid in these days of political correctness, it would be inappropriate for me to use first names, but nonetheless, I'm grateful to you both for the offer. May I get you a cup of tea or coffee before we commence?"

"Thank you, inspector, but we had one at the cafe opposite this building while we waited for the appointed time," said Gill. "So, as you must be very busy and both of us have other things to do, may I suggest we show you our evidence and relay to you our conclusions?"

Unquestionably has all her marbles in action. "Very well, you have my undivided attention. It's in conjunction with a burglary, and you think you can provide evidence on how to solve the crime. Would that be a rough summary of your intent?"

"More than that," said Sheila. "We think we can show you how well-organised these burglaries are."

"Do you indeed?" He glanced at Sandra. "So what do you have to show me?"

Sheila opened a copy of the map of the burglaries she had shown the others at the park, and then the list of names and areas. She explained the list, showing how the dots corresponded to the map. "Our conclusion is that someone on the cruise boat is in league with a gang on shore, and they make arrangements to rob the people while they're on board. Not all of these cases have occurred while the people were on board the cruise ship. Some have happened after they've gone on another cruise. It's possible that they didn't get the complete address whilst on the ship, and it's our conjecture that they must have followed the next victim when they left the ship. Then, when they next go on a cruise, the criminals know the house is empty and break into the property."

Wainwright listened and glanced at the list of areas and the map of the south coast with the numbered dots on it. "Assuming you're right, and I'm not saying you are, how would anyone get the information such as addresses? Information like that isn't just given out to everybody."

"Agreed," said Gill, picking up the question. "But we have dance hosts on board the ship who are charming to any poor ladies who are widows. They ask questions—all-be-it subtle—about our lives now that we're alone. Some are grateful for the dance but aren't forthcoming about their financial and living status. Others speak freely about some things left by their husbands and how they've adapted their lives. Collections of antiques, gold, silver, and all sorts of things are freely talked about in general conversation. We sat at a table and listened to one lady who was saying that she puts all her jewellery in the safe built on the floor and covered by a carpet. It's not that they're boastful; it's because they miss the conversation. And when we get together with people in a similar position then some things that shouldn't be said come out. Should this be overheard, then they could be marked out for further attention. Others ask if anyone has any advice on the disposal of a stamp collection and how to do it to their best advantage."

"And the addresses?"

"One possibility is the future tours desk. We have found that on three, maybe four occasions, a dance host has been near the future tours desk and could have overheard the details."

"But surely they don't need them to state their address. It'd be on their system."

"Yes, but they always need to check who they're dealing with, and the dance host is not staff, so couldn't access the system. The future tour consultant asks what cabin you're in, and then when it comes up, they ask the person to confirm their first line of the home address and their postcode. Once given, they then go into the cruise on offer, knowing they're dealing with a genuine person, but anyone listening in thus has their home address."

"Bit obvious, don't you think? Someone standing nearby, clearly listening in on the conversation."

"Not if it's a semi-staff member who has a right to be in the vicinity. Dance hosts fill in forms for extra duties, things like being a tail-end Charlie to make sure they don't get stray people on the tour. Filling in a form for this would be quite normal and not suspicious."

D.I. Wainwright looked again at the map. "You do realise that a lot of the burglaries on this map are completely out of my jurisdiction, don't you? And what you've given me is not fact but supposition. You think this is the way it's done, but it's not fact. You've amassed a lot of data, and that's to your credit, but as proof, there remains nothing in it that could be called proof. Clearly, I can't go on board cruise ships and arrest anyone who's employed to dance with widows. What could I charge them with? I'm sorry, ladies, but as it is, you have no solid evidence. All you have is a flimsy idea that might be better in a novel. We need solid proof to act on any of it."

"What if we got some more evidence by going on a cruise and dropped a few hints of a suitable treasure held in one of our houses? You could catch them in the act."

D.I. Wainwright looked at the ladies in amazement. "The police funds don't stretch to funding jollies for ladies to go on cruises." He leaned forward. "No, I'm sorry, ladies, but with no foundation to base your theory on about some dancer organising the robberies, I can take no further action. I will, however, file your map and your list of areas, and I'll contact other forces to see if they might like to make a comment. My advice to you both is to leave this to the professionals. My colleague will see you out,. Thank you for your interest." He stood and offered his hand.

The ladies, clearly disappointed, shook his hand and left the room, guided by Sandra.

As they walked to the car park, Gill was almost at the point of shouting out her frustration at the detective. They reached the car, and she then let it go.

Her arms straight down by her sides, her hands clenching and opening she said, "That condescending, insufferable, fat excuse for a policeman. How dare he think we were looking for a free cruise on the police budget? He didn't even give us a chance to explain that we'd already paid for a cruise. He just dismissed us as if we were a nuisance."

"Yes. However, he does have a point," said Sheila as she unlocked the car. "It *is* supposition, not fact. We must act on that, and if we're going to continue, we have to find a way to prove our theory."

Gill looked at her friend. "So, help the professionals even

if they dismiss us as interfering old biddies?"

"Exactly that," said Sheila as she got into the driver's seat. "The best we can do now is give thought to what would constitute proof. One positive point is we know that our main suspect will be sailing with us since he divulged that information to us on our last cruise."

***

D.I. Wainwright looked down on the two ladies as they crossed the road towards the car park. He turned as Sandra returned to his office. "Well, Constable Villiers, that was indeed an interesting visit. We have work to do now, and I'd like to move on this PDQ. We can't have the public feeling they can solve crimes, but I have to say that I wish we had those two on our staff."

"So you didn't feel that it was a lot of fanciful thoughts, as you seemed to imply," said Sandra.

"It *was* all supposition, but they also gave us some positives that might give us leads to solving the outbreak of burglaries we've had in the area. When they mentioned the number of cases in and around Southampton and the high-end theft of furniture and collections, my ears pricked up. That matches some of the cases we've had land on our desk. Now, pull all the cases we've had reported, tally them to the map they provided, and make a list of dates."

"Right, and why don't we use a few of the constables to do some of the cross-referencing on the cruise boat timing, or did you want to do that?"

"Yes, Sandra, that can be done by a couple of our research people. I want sailing dates of arrival and departure of every cruise ship, with the amount of the days for the cruise. Oh, and what cruise line it was. This could be the break we need."

Sandra looked at him. "It would've been nicer to have told those two ladies that we would investigate the possibility that their suppositions had some foundation. Oh, they mentioned the name of a dance host. Shall I get my cross-referencing on him also? It'll mean getting in touch with the central offices of the cruise ships, but they should be able to provide the dates he worked for them and on which cruise ship."

D. I. Wainwright returned to his desk. "I wonder if he has an agent. We don't want to alarm him yet, but if he's a player, then it's better he doesn't know we're making enquiring about him." He looked at her. "And yes, maybe you're right about letting the two old ladies know we took their information seriously, but if we do catch the bad guys, I'll personally seek Gill and Sheila out and thank them. Now get going." And he waved his arm at her as he picked up a new yellow folder to study.

***

After the poor reception they'd from the police, it was Gill who came up with a plan for their hopeful entrapment of the crooks a few weeks later.

The new house would be hers in a week's time and her furniture would be taken down to the house once the work was done that she required. She liked soft muted colours, and all of the rooms were bright and in your face. Offers had been made for her home, but so far, not for the amount she required. With two properties, she could return to her own house, then once the taxi departed, if someone followed her, they would see her go into that house. After a short while, she could leave and go down to her new house.

With most of her furniture removed by then, they could set up cameras inside the old house, and when or if the crooks broke in, they'd get a shock to find there was very little in the house. It might panic them, and they may make a mistake. Sheila would organise the company to install the cameras, and then once that was done, they would need to drop a lure for the dance hosts to overhear. If Gerald Portman was on board as he'd said he would be, then that would be a bonus, but they had no idea how many dance hosts were involved, if they were right.

It was just about thinking up an idea for the host to consider it'd be interesting enough to organise the visit. Sheila solved this after watching *Antiques Roadshow* on the TV. Someone had a collection of watches, the value of which were very high. She had made a note of one then looked it up on the internet. There were lots of different types, but some were a limited production, and she picked one of those.

After downloading a copy and all of the info, she declared to Gill that she thought she had the bait. Both thought this was very exciting and felt they had sorted everything out.

Unfortunately, even the best-laid plans can go wrong.

CHAPTER TWELVE

September

It was almost two months after the talk about the distribution of the gains from their sale when once again, when Robert was waiting to pick up Partner from Dover. This time it was a Saga ship unloading its passengers, and the cruise had resulted in quite a big bag.

He waited for the attendant to start calling names out for the limo drivers to leave the parking area and collect their rides. Robert was dressed in his suit once again, but he had the air-con fully on since it was unseasonably hot outside. It was late in the month, and the weather pundits were calling it an Indian summer. Last week, it had been chucking it down with monsoon-like rain, but this week, temperatures of seventy-eight Fahrenheit. This was Dover, not Delhi.

Ten more minutes went by, before the attendant emerged from his office, which looked more like a shed, and waited until drivers emerged from their vehicles. He called out for the first three cars to pick up Masson, Davies, and Roberts to go down to the yellow zone.

Robert took his cap off and wiped his forehead with a hanky from his pocket. It was a hot and sticky day. *Far too hot to be wearing these togs. Global warming. Indian summers. Why can't we just have rain at night and sunshine during the day, but not this hot?*

Other drivers collected their rides after the attendant had called the names, and as the parking area emptied, Robert still stood, as was expected of him, by the limo. He knew he would be last, but he had to look the part. He fingered his shirt collar trying to ease the cloying, damp neckline. *In this day and age, surely even the posh folk would allow their drivers to dress in a more casual way.* He glanced around and saw most of the drivers were in open-necked shirts and only a few had ties on. *What a stupid bit of material a tie is.*

Again, Partner had messaged for one person to be

followed, and John was already on his motorbike, following the car with Ruth Wilson inside it. At last, Robert was told that he could go on down to the yellow zone to await his ride, who was a little late disembarking.

Robert got back into the car and started the engine. As he drove down to the empty zone, he thought about the items they'd collected from the cruise ship's clients who had supplied so much useful information whilst on board. Partner had been sat at the table next to Ronald Chapman, who was telling a fellow diner about his motorcycle collection. He boasted about the workshop at the bottom of his garden and how he repaired and built motorbikes and vintage bicycles in it. It was a garage that was for two cars, but he'd converted it to his workshop. He was a metal worker, now retired, but still forged parts from the original pieces for replacement.

He had a 1952 K-model Sportster Harley Davidson, two WW2 messenger motorbikes, and a partly rebuilt BSA vintage motorbike that was his latest project.

Robert smiled; he didn't have them now. They'd cleared everything out of the garage. They'd also visited the house and found that his wife, who had kept her mouth shut, was a collector of dolls. Oddments had joined their haul: a 1960s fur coat and two large plant pots complete with plants, likely worth over £2,000 each. Robert couldn't imagine spending that kind of money on a bloody plant, but these people had more money than sense.

The family had some very nice furniture too, but with very little room on the truck once the motorbikes were loaded, they'd had to leave them behind. There was to be no return visit. That was risky and stupid, and Robert wasn't stupid.

He stopped in the yellow zone and waited for Partner to turn up.

He still wasn't comfortable with Gerald. That itch was driving him mad. But yesterday, he had done something about it. He had got in touch with a friend who ran a detective agency and had arranged with him to find out more about Partner. He had given Charlie Evans his partner's name, said he would be bringing him home today, and gave the rough timing for his arrival. Charlie had asked if this was a love interest or a debtor who was being awkward.

Robert told him that he'd booked his car service, but there was something that just didn't sit well with him. He didn't know what it was, but that he'd like him to find out as much as he could about Gerald Masters.

Ten minutes later, Gerald came from the warehouse following a man with his cases loaded onto a trolley. Robert popped open the boot and walked to the back to assist the porter in loading the cases and bags into the car.

Once everything was in the boot, he slammed it shut and watched Partner give the porter a five-pound note through the window. Robert got into the car and pulled away.

"How did the visit to the Chapmans' house go, Robert?"

"Oh, I see. Now that the dust has settled after our little disagreement, I expected something like, 'How are you, Robert? Are you and the lads well?' not straight down to business."

"I must say, you get very cranky when you come to pick me up. Okay, I hope you and the team are well. Now, how did the visit to the Chapmans' house go, Robert?"

"I'm hot and sticky wearing this gear. Most of the other drivers were in shirts and open necks, and there wasn't a tie in sight."

"Ah, the same old gripe. It's either far too cold or too hot."

"Yeh, well. It wouldn't hurt to agree to me wearing an open-necked shirt, and no chauffeur's hat or coat in this weather."

"It would change the whole effect, Robert. Now, the Chapmans' visit."

"I've got an estimate here for the bikes, the parts, and the doll collection. There were a few oddments of furniture as listed, but a tidy sum in the offing," he said as he passed a couple of sheets of paper over his shoulder to Gerald.

Partner was quiet as he looked at the items and the estimates. "You did very well, Robert, if we get the estimates for these things. We'll have a good return for our efforts. £38,000 for the bikes and oddments. Good job you picked those dolls up too. The estimates are fantastic: £2,000 for the native Indian sack doll circa 1800s, and the two nineteenth century Marionette puppets at fifteen hundred each. Then the two walnut pieces of furniture. A mid-Victorian walnut desk, approx. £8,000 and the loveseat estimated at £6,000. Brilliant."

Robert glanced at Partner as he went over the values and the listings in detail, then returned his attention to the driving.

A few hours later, Robert pulled up at Partner's house and got out of the car. Sweat began to pour from Robert's face as the heat hit him. Partner lifted one case out and walked down the pathway to the front door. Robert hauled the other two cases out and dragged them down to the front door. Partner took them one by one and pushed them into the hallway.

"Thank you, Robert. You're looking very hot; get back into your car with the nice cooling air con, and you'll soon feel cool again."

Robert turned and started to walk up the path.

"Take your coat off, Robert, and loosen your tie. That'll help."

Then it hit him. He had never been invited into Partner's house. He'd never even offered him a drink of water. When he reached the car, Robert pulled his coat and tie off and threw them into the back seat.

He looked up and down the road to see if Charlie was nearby, but apart from a man pulling out a length of cable telephone out of a van parked a few doors away, nothing seemed to look as if Charlie was on the job.

I hope Charlie Evans is here somewhere because something isn't right at all.

***

The following week, at a pub outside Guildford, a business meeting was held and the four people, as was customary, discussed the visits made and viewed the updated assessment of prices for the items available for the next black auction. Bookings had been made online and so far, this one was set to exceed expectations for the number of attendees.

Swindon was their next location, and it would be the first time that Robert would get 60% of the take.

After the plates were cleared and the server had moved away, Partner asked, "John, did you manage to follow Ruth Wilson to her home? She'll be one that will be a worthwhile visit. She collects vintage pin cushions."

"Yes, no trouble at all. I've got to say, those houses through Haywards Heath are top-notch. Anyway, it's in Redfield's area and is a detached property. We should be able to reverse up the drive—it's nice and straight—then load and drive out. Couldn't see any alarm systems, but that's not to say there isn't one."

"Excellent," said Partner." He looked at his notes. "Another last-minute one I came across as I was booking a tour job on this last cruise. David and Vivien Walters were booking another cruise, and I overheard the first line of their address and postcode. This is it." He passed Robert the piece of paper with the address written on it. "They go back to the same Fred Olsen boat, but from Southampton. They're both bridge instructors and get discounted bookings as they teach and help others learn the game. I've met them but not spent any time with them. Fred Olsen will pick them up, and they go on the same cruise as me on my next cruise."

Partner paused and looked out the window at the way the trees were shaking as the winds gusted through their branches and lifted the first few leaves, causing them to dance in the air before dropping them down to the ground.

"He was on a tour with me," he said as his attention returned to those sat at the table. "I was acting as a tail-end lookout on a tour, and I overheard him discussing with another passenger about a toy that he wanted to buy from them. He was asking the date of the Star Wars model and whether it was in the box, and then said he would like to see it. He said if it was going to be sold, he would like first call on it." He paused and looked at each of his listeners. "I looked up Star Wars models online and some figures can fetch £2,000."

"For a kid's model of a Star Wars figure? The world has gone mad. What would it have cost when it first came out?" asked Robert.

"Just nine pounds and ninety-nine pence."

There were gasps of amazement.

"So, gentlemen, he must be one who gets a visit from you but make it two or three days after they depart."

"Anything that looks like kids' stuff then," said Badger.

"Not quite. If it looks as if it's loved, looked after, something like that, then lift it. GU28 is Petworth area, but it might be just outside. I'll leave you to sort out the exact address from the info I gave you. Remember, most items will be still in their boxes; look after them, and don't crush them. A damaged box can take £600 off the sale price."

"Well, Partner, if it's hot on the day I drive you to Southampton, I'm not wearing the jacket, cap, or tie. Wearing the full chauffeur's togs, I stand out amongst all the other drivers."

"You know my feelings, but I do understand. Any other things to talk about?"

No one said anything, so Robert got to his feet and went to pay the bill.

Partner left them to it. John and Badger pulled the truck around the front and waited for Robert to come out. With the air-con on, they started on their journey back to the warehouse.

Robert was quiet all the way home, and on arrival, Badger asked, "Is everything okay with you, guv? You've been unusually quiet all the way back?"

"It's fine, Badger. I was just going over the options for the extra visit, but I'll talk to you about my ideas later on. Now, get on home. It's your lucky day. Full pay, short day."

"And a free bit of nosh." Badger closed the door and got back into the truck.

Robert watched him drive away, then went into the warehouse and up to his office.

What the hell has happened to Charlie Evans?

CHAPTER THIRTEEN

October

The day of the start of the cruise came quite quickly, and with the chill winds blowing and autumn colours showing on the leaves, the wind had started to lay a carpet of colour blown from the trees above.

The ship had set a time to arrive and board, and the ladies' driver had timed the pickup and delivery to perfection. They thanked their taxi driver and reminded him that they would text him of the expected disembarking time nearer the end of the cruise.

Their cases were removed and after watching them disappear into the warehouse, they walked the short way to the reception area to check in and receive their boarding pass.

Slowly, they moved forward and reached the check-in desk. Once confirmed that each would like to register their credit card, rather than share, the process of taking a photo to go on the new card continued.

"Why can't you use the photo you had from our last cruise?" asked Gill.

"Well," said the processing clerk, "we don't keep photos from one cruise to another. After two months, they're deleted. As your cruise with us was just over five months ago, we will need a new photo. It's part of the Data Protection Act."

"Oh, thank you for that. Should I smile for this one or take a pose like I did for my passport?"

"Smile. We like to think that you're going to have a great time with us."

After the photo was taken, Gill stepped back with her boarding card in hand, and Sheila took her place. As Sheila answered all the questions about her health, Gill glanced around and spotted their main suspect, waiting to be called up to the desk to have his boarding card issued.

"Well, that's done," Sheila said. "Now we can board, get settled in, and sort out our clothes."

"I've just seen our main suspect waiting to be processed. He's behind me in row eleven," said Gill as Sheila put her papers away.

"Oh, yes. I see him. Right, let's get on board and get settled. We have some practice to do. It's important that this is laid out right to him. He mustn't suspect a thing."

"Yes, Inspector Chancel. I'll try and look casual and uninterested about the fact that he's going to be on board."

Sheila grinned. "Granny sleuths, we may be, but a force to be reckoned with, as he's going to find out."

They made their way on board, then headed to their room. Once in the room, they sorted out the wardrobe section, each taking part of it for their dresses and the cupboards for each to put their bits in. They used the time to unpack and hang or store in the cupboards they were using. This was done in relative silence, save for one asking the other for a hanger, or could they pass something to them. It had become a routine that worked well for them.

When they were settled and had pushed the empty cases under the beds, Gill put the kettle on, and Sheila drew out a small folder from her hand luggage.

With the tea made, they sat down and Gill said, "Now we have our cup of tea, Inspector Chancel, shall we go over the way we're going to drop the hook in front of our suspect?"

"Sit down, Inspector Blakeney," said Sheila, "and I'll run over a few of the salient points to this sting."

***

Robert had watched his partner go into the reception area as the last of his cases went onto a conveyor belt to go onto the cruise ship. He'd still not received word from Charlie Evans, and his itch was still causing him grief.

He thought about his next house visit to be made, once Partner confirmed that the bridge teachers, David and Vivian Walters, were on board. It was a boring game in Robert's opinion, but some seemed to like playing it. The Walters couple got a free cruise as instructors when they taught guests how to play it, so it was a win-win for them.

Today he was happy to have the chauffeur gear on. It wasn't exactly cold, but the weather was gearing up for the winter period. *How quickly the year seems to have gone.* Robert got back into the car and drove out through the docks to the main road that would take him back home.

***

Gerald Portman hadn't noticed the two ladies as they checked in. He was still preoccupied with his thoughts on the discussion with Robert. Gerald had been taken aback by the response to his threat to Robert. He'd wrongly thought that it would make him withdraw his demand for a bigger slice of the money. He didn't actually know any rough types of people—that had been a bluff and a wrong one. Robert had called it and turned it around so that he had to capitulate and agree on the reduction in his take. He may have been playing the same card of a threat, but Gerald felt that if either of them did have a chance to play rough, Robert would have the contacts.

He had done a little research on Robert before he contacted him about the new venture. The word had been that he sailed close to the wind and did now and then cross the line into illegal dealings, but that he was a clever man, who always stayed clear of the police. There'd been no mention of any rough stuff. *Maybe it's time to re-think this partnership.*

Gerald boarded the ship and went to his cabin he was sharing with Mark Wilson, a dance host he had shared with before. Like him, Mark was a clean and tidy guy and quite a reasonable dancer who took his share of dancing with the ladies. Both had respect for each other.

Mark was unpacking and greeted Gerald with a wide smile. "I'm glad I get to share with you, Gerald. I've taken the same bed I had last time we were together and started using the same space we used last time. It makes life easier doing that, doesn't it?"

Gerald thanked him and started to unpack his suitcase.

"We're on duty this evening, so it's dark blue trousers and white shirts," Mark said. "Darren Baker and his wife are the lead hosts. I think you may've been with them at some time in the past. They seem a regular team leader set."

Gerald folded his trousers over a hanger and hung them in the wardrobe. "Yes, but only once. I've only been working with Fred Olsen cruise lines for about two years and Saga for four."

"Ah, yes. I've been doing this for five years now with the Olsen ships and six with Saga."

Gerald placed his pants and socks into a drawer. "Six years? Is it that long since your wife died?"

"Seven and a half. It took me a year to realise that I had to change my life. I would never find another woman like Wendy, but now I can go on dancing, not with many who have any finesse as she did, but it gives me something to hang on to. And it pleases me that others are getting some pleasure from my attempts to dance with them." He looked at Gerald taking out his jackets and hanging them ready to go into the wardrobe. "How about you? You said you'd tell me your story the next time we shared a room. Last time I asked, you said it was a little too raw for you to talk, but you must be through the rough bit now and be able to talk about it."

Gerald panicked. He had no prepared story and did a quick search in his mind for a suitable one. "Yes," he said, "I suppose it is. My story isn't as tragic as yours. I was engaged to be married to a girl who had a high-powered job. Top of her field, actually, but then she informed me that her parents said that I wasn't quite who they felt their daughter should be thinking of marrying. So she returned my ring."

Mark folded his socks up to go into his drawer. "Blimey, mate, that's a bit rough in this day and age."

Gerald was quite pleased with his story so far and that he'd embellished his tale with a small amount of fact from his recent encounter with Helen Prescott. He nodded and put on a sad face. "I begged her not to listen to her parents, but she was adamant that it was for the best. She insisted that I collect my things from her flat and not bother her again. I moved out, and she blocked my calls. Within a year, an announcement in *The Times* stated that she was engaged to some up-and-coming politician called Thomas. His father was something big in the business world, and that was it."

He looked at Mark, who was looking crestfallen at Gerald's sad story.

Pleased with the way it was going, Gerald continued, "My depression took me to the lowest levels. I got drunk and realised that she was not going to be mine, and her love for me was not as deep as mine for her. I loved her as a future wife, but she just loved me for the sexual gratification I could give her." He was very pleased with the last part of his story. It was a stroke of genius turning Helen's part of the story around to make it sound like *he'd* been used.

"So no new woman in your life either?" Mark asked.

"No, Mark. It'll take a long time for me to want to look at another eligible young woman."

"And they say it's a man's world. It's nothing without a woman as part of it, is it?"

Gerald kept his expression solemn, "No." He left it like that. Once a successful story is told, let it be.

They finished their unpacking and checked the times they would start their duty. The first appointment would be with the two main hosts, the entertainment manager, and any other dance hosts that had joined the cruise.

"Time for a cup of tea before we get the usual briefing." Mark closed the wardrobe door and went to the sideboard with the tea-making equipment laid out.

Robert smiled. A cup of tea sounded perfect. Something civilised to make the world a better place.

***

Sheila ran over the items on the list once again. "It's going to be awkward to 'accidentally' let him know that you have a collection of watches that belonged to your husband if you know nothing about them."

"But surely, if it was my husband's collection, I wouldn't necessarily know much or anything about them," said Gill.

"That's the point. You must have some knowledge to be able to drop the hint. You can't just go up to him and say, 'My husband collected watches of some considerable value.

Fancy robbing me?' Can you?"

"Well, I know that. But it's the name and type that seem to be so important. Are you sure that an underwater watch is worth a lot of money? We can't be sure that he'll know that."

"If he's the professional thief we think he is, we must assume that he knows most things worth a lot of money. We don't know that it's him, but we've agreed that we'll tempt him first and see if he shows any interest. He told us that he might be on this cruise, and he is. If we get the info out to him by accident, then we can sit and wait to see what happens. In the meantime, get studying this picture of the watch in question."

Gill looked at the sheet. "Omega Seamaster Diver Chronometer men's watch! Do you really think I'm going to remember that mouthful?"

"No, but Omega diver's watch might do the trick," Sheila said, sounding frustrated.

"Oh, I think I might be able to remember that."

CHAPTER FOURTEEN

October

Detective Inspector Wainwright sat at his surprisingly tidy desk and smiled as he reread the missive from his counterpart covering the south coast to Dover. Detective Inspector Harris had messaged him after his enquiry about robberies that could be associated with cruise ships.

Since the visit by the two ladies to inform him of their suspicions of an organised gang masterminded by someone on a cruise ship, he'd been digging deeper with the help of his team. Other cases had come in, and this latest message from his colleague in the Southeast division confirmed that they also could link a lot of their reported thefts to a cruise ship. Worse, they even had a riverboat cruise that had also had a couple robbed while they were cruising.

Now he had another on his desk that had been dug up from the search. This one was in Kings Barton, near Winchester. Tracy McCall had reported the break-in after her return from a cruise in March. He looked at the list submitted to the insurance company and shook his head. The items that were listed only had a small value compared to some he had found, but nevertheless, it was just as upsetting.

The gang were certainly selective,: a 1930s oak hat, coat, umbrella, and walking stick hall stand. Value £165.00. An oak gateleg dropleaf table, valued at £495.00. Then came the lower-end things like the coffee-making machine and plasma TV, which cost a lot to buy new but were worth very little second-hand. Leather coat. *Completely out of fashion now.* Cigarette cards mounted in books. No value was detailed but they could have been a higher amount. Wine and spirits, silver and gold items. A Victorian musical box with no value submitted. The woman had simply put it on the claims form, with no idea of its monitory value. It had been a gift from her husband and was lost forever. There was a silver tea set that had been passed to her from her mother. That was most likely melted by now. Necklaces and her iPad and laptop.

What had attracted them to this house for these slim pickings?

His chair moaned as he sat forward placed the list in the folder and looked at Mrs McCall's cruise dates. Did the name of the dance host once again occur on those dates? That had been on the granny sleuth's list but needed checking.

What was perplexing was the number of cases the ladies had given him that had already been matched with the dance host's presence. But it didn't really prove anything. It could all just be a big coincidence.

The stupid thing was, he realised, he was almost rooting for them to be right.

***

Charlie Evans had contacted Robert saying he had some interesting and shocking news for him about the said Gerald Masters.

When Charlie came to see Robert, he was ushered upstairs to his home, and Robert made sure the do not disturb note was placed on the outside of the door. Charlie sat down in the armchair, and Robert sat down in the chair opposite him.

Charlie opened his briefcase and pulled out some papers.

Who the hell uses a briefcase nowadays? I hope I haven't made a mistake with him.

Charlie cleared his throat and looked at Robert. "I watched you arrive with the passenger you know as Gerald Masters."

"What? I looked for you, but you weren't anywhere to be seen."

"I was in plain sight. I was the telephone engineer just down the road."

"But you had your back to us working with some cable."

"Yes, that's correct. You see, my camera was pointing up the road, and I was looking into a small screen watching everything."

"Oh, you sneaky bugger. So what happened after I left."

"I started to pack up the cable and was closing the doors when your gentleman came from the house, looked up and down the road, and then opened his garage door."

"To get his run-around out?"

"No, to get his Mercedes Benz coupé out. That's a car worth £50k minimum, and it was last year's registration."

I'm going to have to reduce his profits a lot more if he can afford to blow them on a car like that. Robert's eyes flashed this way and that as the information filtered through. "I'm listening, Charlie. This news is quite a shock."

"Better get the whisky out then, Robert," said Charlie as he placed another page in front of himself. "I followed him and then asked my partner to take over the tail. David followed him to a very large house in the country. His real name is Gerald Portman, according to the man David asked who was working in the garden. The house belonged to his friend Fredrick Winterbottom, a politician of some note who buys paintings and other collectables. Mr Portman is a regular visitor.

Gerald Portman is the well-respected son of Sir Arthur Portman, a well-known import/exporter. He made his money buying things in house clearance and then selling them on. He now has companies making things for him, which he sells direct to outlets home and abroad."

"I knew something was wrong, but this? Why did he lie?" Robert was very unsettled.

"Gerald Portman went to university to study fine arts and got a distinction at Northumbria University. He also studied for and achieved his Graphic Design BA Honours. He took a commission in the Army as a reservist. I didn't bother to dig deeper. There seemed no point now you have this info about him. If you want me to dig deeper, say the word."

Why the hell is he a common con artist with all that behind him?

"The name you know him by is a man who died in Africa during the rebellions when the locals killed any white people living over there. He was a soldier sent over there to help with the evacuation of British nationals. He returned in a coffin."

Robert got up, went to the drinks cabinet, and took out a newly claimed whisky bottle. It wasn't as good as his last bottle, but even the best would taste sour with this sort of news. He poured one for each of them. He sipped a small amount and let it slide around his mouth before swallowing it down.

Charlie said nothing and simply watched Robert pace this way and that.

"None of this is making sense," Robert said. *Why would someone with so much money behind them become a petty thief?* It was a question that Robert couldn't ask out loud, but so many questions rushed through his mind as he continued to pace backwards and forwards.

Charlie finished his whisky and stood. "I'll leave you my paperwork and arrange my bill to be sent to you, Robert. I know you're upset with my findings, and I don't know why nor do I need to. If you want any more info gathering, please give me a call. Thanks for the drink, Robert. Shall I see myself out?"

"Eh. Oh, sorry, Charlie. No, I'll come with you and see you out. You've done very well. I'll get Badger to drop a cheque to you once you've sent your bill."

"Thanks, Robert. I appreciate that."

Once Charlie had left, Robert closed the door and latched it. There was still one removal van to return later this evening. Now he had to think this info through.

***

The ladies didn't meet up with their target dance host until three days into the cruise.

They'd intended to go up to the observation deck, where there was a reasonable dance floor, but other things had come up. Come up, literally! Making the crossing over the Bay of Biscay had been rough, and both Sheila and Gill felt under the weather, taking it in turns to rush to the bathroom.

They emerged slightly shaky once the passage became easier and had their first small bite to eat, porridge being the best option for a weakened stomach. By lunchtime, both had perked up a bit and still staying light, had a ham roll and a cup of tea to help it down.

Gaining their old vigour by the evening, they were ready for their first cooked meal in the dining room and found that others on the table had fared just as badly. It was reassuring to know they weren't the only poor sailors.

They finished their meal and, not feeling any adverse effects, made their way up to the observation room for the chance of a dance to round off the day at sea. They sat at a table and were joined by another lady who introduced herself to them as Vicki Owen. She explained that this was her first cruise and her first holiday since her husband had died.

Gill and Sheila explained they were in a similar situation. They assured her that once she started to move around and ate on tables reserved for single people, she would soon find people who she'd met before, and it wouldn't be quite as hard.

They ordered their drinks and waited for the dance team to arrive. Small talk went on between the ladies, and they found out that Vicki came from Durrington, near Worthing along the A27 towards Brighton. They exchanged the area they lived in and changed the subject quickly to her dancing.

After about ten minutes, the two people dance co-ordinators arrived, and three men also arrived, one of them being Gerald Portman. The dance couple introduced themselves as Darren and Gloria and then introduced the dance hosts, Mark, Gerald, and Raymond to any ladies who wanted to dance but had no partner.

They started with a sequence dance, and Mark asked Gill to dance with him. Sheila waited to be asked. Competition for a dance partner was going to be high, with a total of eight women indicating they wanted to dance.

Sheila watched the couples dance around the floor, enjoying the music, her feet tapping in time, and her body swaying. Other couples had joined in, and the floor was quite packed. The next dance was a ballroom quickstep, and Mark asked her to join him on the floor. She was whisked around the floor, reminding her of the time when Graham would take her in his arms and sweep her around the ballroom. It was a sad fact that more ladies outlived their husbands, and that was evident in the number of ladies sitting watching her now.

She returned to her table after thanking her partner for the dance, and the next dance was announced. Neither of the ladies were asked, but Vicki was, by Gerald.

As the music started, Sheila turned to Gill. "Vicki looks as if she's a good dancer. Quite light on her feet."

"Mark is okay, but he's not as good as Gerald," Gill said.

The hours of dancing were slowly drawing to an end, and in that time, Gill hadn't danced with Gerald Portman once, but Sheila had.

She had started by saying as they had danced, "I'm sure you wouldn't remember us, but we have met before."

Robert frowned, then asked a few questions about their last meeting. Sheila told him when it had been and a little bit about the cruise destinations.

As they danced, he remained quiet, the frown deepening as he cast his mind back. Then his face lit up as he remembered and said, "Wasn't there something about a lady receiving a message that someone had died?"

"No," Sheila said, correcting him. "It was someone who had their home burgled whilst on the cruise."

"Yes, I seem to remember that. A sad affair. People robbing others whilst they are on holiday is a terrible thing."

He escorted her to her chair, and she waited for the next dance.

The dancing session finished, and the three ladies left to go to the show due to start in a short while.

Tomorrow was another day, and maybe then, Gill would get the chance to drop the bait.

*** *

Robert was still unsettled but had a visit to organise to David and Vivien Walters, the bridge teachers on the cruise ship Partner was currently on. He didn't know if he wanted to continue with the arrangement, but in the end, arranged the visit for the following evening.

Everything went well, and Robert came back with a lorry filled with goodies. A small Georgian English elm bureau that had a receipt in the drawer informing him it was circa

1720. The receipt also gave the price paid as £6,800, and the amount they should insure it for, which was £8,000.

Robert thought that was most helpful of the Walters family and hoped they *did* get it insured. Also inside the drawers were lots of boxes with silver Vesta cases in them. The value would be low, but anything from thirty quid up all added to the tally.

The spare bedroom was the treasure chest. There were toys in boxes and some on shelves all around the room. Robert found a book with each one listed, along with the price paid. That went into his pocket as he supervised the packing of the toys into cardboard boxes to load onto the lorry.

They took wine, the TV, and a very nice hearth rug, as was the small cabinet by the armchair, which Robert found opened at the top, and a drinks unit lifted itself up for the person in the chair to sort out their drink. Better still, he found a sixteen-year-old malt whisky in it. That was definitely coming home with him, and the cabinet would be placed next to Robert's easy chair for him to relax while he enjoyed his new whisky. There was no way it would be going into the auction.

He fondled the bottle and looked at the label. The Aberlour Speyside single malt whisky must have cost David Walters over a hundred quid, and he'd left almost four-fifths of it for Robert to appreciate.

Once all of that was packed into the back of the lorry, they set off on their way back. They would unload everything into the new rental container, then continue to Robert's home, where the new addition to his home comforts would be taken up the stairs. Badger would then return home with the empty lorry.

Once Robert had seen everything unloaded and placed into the container, he locked it up, and once they got to the warehouse, he placed the new addition exactly where he wanted it. Once Badger was on his way home, he relaxed in his chair, pressed the top of his new serving toy, and poured himself a small sample of the newly acquired malt whisky.

He lifted his glass. "Cheers, Mr. Walters," he said and took his first sip.

CHAPTER FIFTEEN

October

The two ladies were enjoying the cruise, rough seas had abated, and as they made their way down the Portuguese coast, the sun came out.

Excitement had occurred when the passengers were told that a pod of dolphins were swimming at the bow and jumping through waves as the ship cut through the water.

Sheila was getting frustrated with the lack of opportunities to drop the bait into the suspect's hearing, but a new idea was forming in her brain. She just needed Gill to go along with the plan. They'd arrived at a port of call this morning, and no dancing would happen in the evening. Some tours would be late returning.

They were aware that tours had been arranged, and it was quite usual for the dance hosts to be asked to accompany the tour guide as a tail-end chaperone to watch over the guests as they followed their leader giving information over his microphone. Gill and Sheila had declined any tours from this port, but they had watched as their suspect joined a tour and followed the group to board the coach.

When you return, mister, thought Sheila as she watched him board the coach, then my bait will be dropped into your lap, and then we'll see what happens.

The morning drifted by at a leisurely pace. They left the ship and walked the short way into Cartagena, a walled city in Spain being their first port of call. They had been there several times in the past, and although it was nice to stretch their legs in the sunshine, with temperatures rising by eleven o'clock, they turned and made their way back.

After a light lunch on board, they watched the tours coming and going throughout the rest of the day from the rear of the ship. Here, they could stay in the shade, air their swimming costumes, and read a book.

By evening, the ladies had freshened up, had a quick

shower, and a change of dress before they went to the dining room. They sat at the same table and exchanged a few words with some of the fellow ladies who were already there. As others came, so did Vicki Owen, who sat next to Gill.

There was lots of talk about the tours, and Gill and Sheila listened to Vicki as she told them about the tour she was on. It seems she had shared the company of that nice dancer who was on duty as an assistant escort to make sure no one strayed from the tour. "Such a nice man. He was most attentive to all of the tourists but spent more time talking to me as we walked around the Roman ruins," she said.

Sheila and Gill said nothing to Vicki about the nice man, but if they were proven right, that nice man might meet D.I. Wainwright soon.

Once the meal was over, the ladies made their way up to the piano room to sit and listen to light music until it was time for the show. They saw Gerald Portman coming along towards them and, seeing Vicki, he stopped and spoke to the three of them.

"Good evening, ladies. I trust you've had a good day." He turned to Gill and Sheila. "Did you do any touring whilst we were at port?"

"No," Gill said. "We just strolled around the city, reacquainting ourselves with a few places we visited before. Not a lot has changed since we came with our husbands, and we've been here a few times since we linked up to continue cruising."

"Good for you. I'm right, aren't I? You were the ladies I met before, and we danced together on another cruise."

Sheila looked at Gill briefly. "Yes, we spoke about the unfortunate lady who had her holiday ruined when someone broke into her house and stole a lot of her treasures that were her memories of her husband."

"Oh, yes. Such a sad state of affairs when one can't go on holiday without that happening. I wonder if they caught the man. I guess we'll never know."

"Well, I can answer that as Martina became friends with us. No one was caught, but the police say they'll keep looking."

Gerald smiled. "Of course they say that, but it's more likely they have no hope of catching the perpetrators of the crime."

"We can only hope they do find a lead. I'd hate them to break into my home and take my husband's collection of watches. I, just like Martina, can't get my head around selling them on. They meant so much to him, especially the deep-sea watch that he always liked to show other collectors."

"Really. Watches, eh? I've never heard of people collecting watches. Cameras, yes, but not watches. What's so special about watches? After all, they aren't period pieces, are they?"

"No," said Gill, "but I seem to remember him saying that it was the number the company made that made them collectable."

"Wasn't it something about the depth it could withstand?" asked Sheila, grinning at Gill.

Gerald is sniffing the bate and feigning a lack of knowledge on the subject. Well done, Gill.

"Ah, yes." Gerald gathered his thoughts. before speaking again. "I wonder if it was made by that company who adopted the twenty-fourth and final letter in the Greek alphabet. Omega watches became the world's best of the best in deep water designs. What an interesting subject, Mrs Blakeney. One learns something new every day."

"Please, call me Gill, and I'm sure if you remember when we met on our last cruise, both Sheila and I asked you to address us by our first names."

"Thank you, I'll remember that when we dance together on another day."

They watched him as he walked away, both wanting to say something but aware of Vicki's presence.

***

Gerald walked away from the three women. He had thought that he might cultivate Vicki to see if she was a prospect, but what a fantastic accident to come up with a gift like that. Omega deep water watches… He remembered one going for quite a big sum in an auction house, and a speed master watch went for fifty grand. And now this old lady had a whole collection of them going to waste. *I mustn't let her or her friend think I'm interested.*

He reached his cabin down in the bowels of the ship and lay down on his bunk. Fortunately, Mark wasn't there, so he settled down to do some research on his laptop. Gerald typed in Omega deep sea watches and gasped at the results. The lowest was twenty thousand and others were above forty thousand. The moon watch was advertised at fifty thousand pounds, but there was a waiting list for that rare item.

He closed his laptop and placed it back in its case. Laying back on the bed, he thought about this new prospect and licked his lips. His phone buzzed, and he pulled it from his jacket pocket. Gerald read the message from Robert telling him that the visit to the card player's house had been crossed from the list and to be prepared to hear the bad news. Gerald deleted the message, lay back on his bed, closed his eyes and smiled.

Another perfect crime had been committed.

***

Sheila and Gill stayed with Vicki, quietly reading their books and having the occasional short conversation until it was time to make their way to the show.

As they sorted out their odd things, Vicki said she was going to stay and join a ladies' team for the quiz. Once the ladies were clear, they let the pent-up words come tumbling out.

"Well, Gill, you played that very well. An Oscar-winning performance."

"He did jump in on the fact that it was a deep-sea watch, didn't her?" said Gill with a smirk.

"Now we have to wait to see if he's taken the bait."

"Lots of small talk. How lovely it is to be able to dance with someone who knows how to."

"Oh, yes, play on his conceit," said Sheila as they reached the theatre. "He thinks that they've out-foxed the police, but he hasn't reckoned on us."

"Super sleuths."

"I think that's a little strong, Gill. We haven't got him yet or proved that it is indeed him that's masterminding a gang of ruffians. Let's say granny sleuths; it feels like that's more in keeping with our image."

"Granny sleuths it is then. Pity, I was enjoying the detective inspector persona. Oh, well."

They went into the theatre to watch the show and each sat quietly with their thoughts until the show started. The ship slipped her moorings and left Cartagena as the ladies watched the presentation on the theatre stage. After two days at sea, they would arrive the following morning in the Tuscany city of Livorno, Italy. But until then, the dancing evenings would once again start.

***

A soft breeze caressed the two ladies as they lay on their loungers reading their books. They had carefully placed the loungers side by side and in opposite directions so they could see each other and everything else that was going on. They had felt that this was a clever idea and were quite excited to see if their suspect would seek them out.

Gill found it difficult to concentrate on her book. She'd read one line and then would look up and around. Sheila seemed more interested in her book, much to Gill's annoyance. "I can't focus on the storyline of this book. My mind is on our will he, won't he visit us question. Do you think he'll come?"

"I don't know, but just read your book, relax, and forget him. The next move is his, and his alone, and agonising over it isn't going to bring him to our loungers."

Gill looked at her friend as she returned to her book. *She's right, but why can't the man just come here if he's going to and help settle my nerves? If it wasn't before one o'clock, I'd have a brandy to calm me down.*

As she picked up her book and opened the page, she saw him come through the doorway and start walking towards them. She kept her head down, looking at the page, but keeping a sideways eye on their approaching suspect.

As he neared them, Gill looked up at him and caught his eye, but he simply nodded and said, "Ladies." He passed by them to disappear through the doors at the other end.

"Well," said Gill in a huff, "not a hesitation at all. A nod, and then he was gone."

Sheila, who had also now put her book down and sat quietly for a while, thinking.

"Well, are you just going to sit there saying nothing? Does that mean we have the wrong man in our sights?"

Sheila smiled. "No. I think he's playing it cool, showing us that he's not interested in the mundane conversation. He's waiting for other information to come to him through you or other sources."

"So what happens now?"

"Nothing. We read our book, enjoy the holiday, and relax."

Gill looked at Sheila as she lay back on the lounger and started to read her book. "Well, you're the cool one. I think the sleuthing business has brought out another you. Wasn't there a song called that?"

Sheila put her book down on her lap. "Yes, almost, I think it was the Seekers, and the song was 'I'll Never Find Another You.' I remember shuffling around with a boyfriend to it."

"Pity they don't ask those sorts of questions in the quiz. We'd win if they did." Gill sank back onto the lounger and silence between them signalled that the conversation was over.

***

Gerald had seen the two women laying on the sun loungers, and at the last minute, he decided that to engage in a conversation with them about the watch collection would be a little suspicious, so he'd just walked on by.

Something was niggling him, and he didn't know what. He examined the conversation once again but could find nothing that didn't sound anything other than accidental information, and these old women could hardly be police.

That Sheila woman—it was most likely her that was causing him to be unsettled. At every encounter, she reminded him about the theft from that Kincade woman's house. Perhaps he should ask how her friend was adjusting after the theft. Showing a little sympathy might sort out his restlessness.

CHAPTER SIXTEEN

October

The sun had shone every morning as the cruise ship sailed to its ports of call around the foot of Italy. They had visited Livorno, then the following day stopped at an impossible place to pronounce correctly but was an ideal stop for tours to Rome.

Contact with the suspect had been poor. He had danced on the two evenings with both Sheila and Gill, but the conversation had been mundane.

"Do you both belong to a dance club?"

"How is your friend who had a burglary whilst on a cruise getting on? So tragic."

"What sort of work did you do after leaving school?"

"Do you only go on Fred Olsen's cruise ships?"

"Have you tried Saga?"

Nothing suspicious, but annoyingly not the questions they both wanted to hear.

Now, there was no dancing on the evening because of lots of tours arriving late back to the ship. Being philosophical and unflinching in the face of the disappointment, they refused to break their silence whenever they came into the presence of Gerald and trusted that somewhere along the line, he would have to ask some questions about the watch collection if he was indeed the ringleader.

But the silence was killing them. Self-doubt began to creep into their minds, enhanced by the nonchalant way he appeared, always so relaxed and calm. Maybe he wasn't the ringleader because he doesn't seem to be interested enough to follow up with questions. It was as if he didn't care about the information.

It was while the ship was going through the straits of Messina that the news came to the two ladies that the bridge card instructors' home had been broken into. Discussions were taking place about the replacement of the teachers, but once David and Vivien Walters had spoken to their family and had been assured that the house had been made secure, they decided to complete the cruise.

Hardly a welcoming message just as they were arriving to visit Venice, a place that both the ladies were looking forward to reacquainting themselves with, but also for the Walters' couple, who had honeymooned there a long time ago.

Vicki had passed this information to them after a conversation during a game of bridge for beginners. She had said how nice they were, and how they had made her and a few others, who had no idea about the game, welcome.

So, another break-in, but how could it be laid at Mr. Portman's door?

They saw very little of Gerald Portman once they docked near to Venice. Gill and Sheila had arranged to join another couple who were going onto the "People Mover," an overhead railway system that would take them to the outskirts of Venice. They'd used this transport before, so they would show them the way, help with the ticket, and then they could go their own ways. For one euro each way, it was the most convenient way to visit since cruise ships were forbidden to move up the Grand Canal.

It was a hot day, but by walking quickly over the connecting bridge from the bus and train station, they were soon in the shade of the narrow pathways that made Venice such a go-see place. Gill and Sheila relished the hustle and bustle of the throngs of people, all going somewhere, stopping to take a picture of this or that. The excitement in their voices told them that this was most likely their first time in this magical, romantic place.

They paused now and then to drink water. Even in the shade, the temperature was causing them to slow their pace. Eventually, they came to St. Paul's square, and once again, the ladies thought of times past when they had stood and looked at the pigeons being fed by tourists who, like them, had bought bags of seed to scatter for the birds.

Choosing the shaded side, they decided to stop and have a cup of coffee, a thing that most tourists want to do, even despite the knowledge that one might need to take out a mortgage to cover the cost. Having rested, they cut through more narrow lanes and came to the Bridge of Sighs. It was said that the view from the bridge was the last sight of Venice convicts saw before their imprisonment.

Now, sightseeing over for the moment, they sought out a place to have a bite to eat, and once they found one and settled into their seats. Once both were comfortable, then the joys of the menu could be examined. They chose a sharing platter and a glass of red wine. As they picked a morsel from the platter, the subject of the bridge instructors again came up. David and Vivien Walters were on the ship, and they were treated almost like staff, as was Gerald Portman, so what was the connection?

As they picked and chewed and sipped the blood red wine, still no answer came.

Then Sheila picked up a large slice of ham and waved it about. "It must've been the last cruise they were on together. They booked this cruise, and he must have been nearby and overheard the dates and their address." She took a bite of the ham as Gill put her glass of wine down.

"Well, I'm glad you decided to eat that piece of ham; I think you aired it quite well before trying it. But I agree, there's no other way it could've been done, and that means he knew that once the ship sailed, he could instruct his cronies to burglarise the Walters' home."

"Assuming," said Sheila as she picked up a small piece of cheese and placed it onto a small portion of the bread, "that he is the gang leader and not an innocent dance host." She then took a bite and watched her friend mull over her words.

"We can't be wrong, surely," said Gill. "It fits. Damn the man. Why can't he just ask me the question and put us out of our misery?"

***

Gerald had to join another touring group while the ship was in Venice. He kept an eye on all of the guests and ushered the passengers along trying to make sure that none made a break for it and tried to escape. The tour was to discover the centuries-old art of glassblowing on the island of Murano. They had gone to the Colleoni Glass Factory and watched a master craftsman shape molten glass.

He'd seen it all before, but it was a small price to pay when he was fishing for information. Future clients were more relaxed on tours, and if it involved alcohol at some point, then information could be gleaned quite easily. Saying things like, "You may as well enjoy it now. Once we get back to our homes, it's back to the old routine unless you're proposing to sell the family fortune and come on another cruise?"

So often, a laugh would follow and then a comment. It had happened two days ago from Mrs. Shellforth who had said, "It would take a miracle to get George to part with his wooden printing blocks. He's collected them for years. He makes one print from them on his old printing machine in the garden shed, then puts it in a shoe box and numbers it. I ask you, what's the point of that?"

"Some are so rare now," George had said, "that people are paying me to print a copy for them. Maureen doesn't realise that some of my early Japanese ones are worth a small fortune, but I couldn't part with them. I'll never sell them. Never!"

"See what I mean?"

"Yes," Gerald had said, "but I also understand that if it gives your husband pleasure, then why stop it? A man or woman who collects things from the past is doing a service to future generations who will be able to view those things one day."

Maureen was silent for a while. "I'd never thought about it like that, so thank you."

No, thank you, he had thought.

He had wandered around behind the guests as they watched the glass-blowing demo going on, but no conversation was likely to be of interest when they were so engrossed in the events before them. He paused his roaming, sat in a chair behind them, and pulled out his phone. He flicked through the messages to see if Robert had picked up the information he'd sent about George Shellforth, and there it was.

Will do the usual with our motorbike friend and will be waiting for instructions. Your message to follow for my pick-up time.

Good old Robert. All the replies were in a sub-message and to an outside eye, wouldn't look suspicious. And now the deep-sea watch or watches. What shall I do about that?

***

While Gerald pondered his next move against Gillian Blakeney, she was busy talking through possibilities with Sheila as to how Gerald could have arranged the theft of the Walters' home.

They were strolling along the canal bank, slowly heading back towards where the station was to return to the ship.

"Let's think about our bait for the moment," said Sheila as they went single file over a narrow canal, pausing only to watch a gondolier pass below them.

"Okay. But he knows I have a collection of watches. The collection presupposes that while the ace in the pack, the diver's watch, is mega money, the rest of the collection may also amount to as much again. He has nothing else."

They paused as they stood sideways on for a group of young people to pass them to a chorus of thankyous.

"No," said Sheila, "but that knowledge would spur him on to pick up as much information as he can about where you live. Because if you lived in Manchester, then there'd be no point."

"Well, I'm sure he's picked up that I'm no Mancunian."

Sheila smiled. "Well, it does come out from time to time, but I don't hold anything against you. It's just part of you, and as a package, you'll do."

Gill looked at Sheila and grinned: the battle was on. "I'll do? And you wonder why I only offer you one glass of wine when you visit my poor abode. I'm very aware of your alcohol problem, but you give me no thanks for trying to keep you on the straight and narrow. My Northern blood forgives you."

They both laughed as they came from the narrow lane out

into a plaza and stopped to look at the buildings surrounding the open space.

"If ever I wanted to uproot my life and move to somewhere else, it would be here. Look at this place. Everywhere you look, there's beauty."

Gill looked at Sheila. "But you'd miss my Northern hospitality, not to mention the glass of wine."

Sheila smiled and took in as much as she could of her surroundings. The two ladies stood in the shade of the buildings behind them, but most of the plaza was bathed in sunlight, bringing the colours of the buildings to life and causing shadows on the carved figures to stand out as a relief.

Before they started again on their way to the station, Sheila said, "If, once I was established here, you wanted to visit me, you could always bring your one-third bottle of wine with you, and we could drink it together on my balcony as we watched the world go by."

"Very well then. Until you move, I will maintain my vigil on your wayward drinking habits and help you to stay on the wagon."

Sheila curtseyed. "I wonder where that expression came from: on the wagon. Another of those questions we may get in a quiz," she said as they started crossing the plaza to take another narrow pathway that followed the Grand Canal.

"Well, I can answer that," said Gill. "Originally, on the water wagon or on the water cart referred to carts used to hose down dusty roads in the 1900s in America. The temperance movement over there put the suggestion that a person who is 'on the wagon' is drinking water rather than alcoholic beverages. Like a lot of worthy sayings, it travelled over to England."

"Well, I hope that question comes up sometime in the future in our quizzes. At least we'll get one right."

They followed the canal and eventually came out to the plaza where the bus and train stations were.

As they paused to make sure of the safest route to the people mover train system, Sheila said, "I've been thinking."

"About the move out to here?"

"No, although it's a pity it's a daydream. I was thinking

about Mr Portman."

"Oh, and have you got a possible answer?"

"Yes, I think I have. Or maybe part of it. He has the information that you have something of value, so why bother to put his subject of interest on a watchful eye, when he can take another easier route? All he has to do is arrange for someone to follow us when we leave the ship, and they have our address."

"Brilliant. It's so obvious. So when we get off the ship, you're expecting someone to follow us home. I shouldn't think it would be a car. They could have problems following us with all the coming and going in the port area. It's more likely to be a motorbike." Gill took a deep breath to calm her excitement. "Goodness, we are clever sleuths."

"Not yet. We need to work out how they know when to rob us, and how they know what car to follow."

Gill looked at Sheila, her mouth dropping open, then said, "Well, the obvious thing to do is sit outside of our house and wait, but that's not going to happen, so he must get some idea while we're on board."

"Yes, exactly, but how can he do that if we don't book another cruise while on board the ship?"

They continued to the people mover station. Using their ticket, they entered through the gate and climbed the steps to the train above. Boarding the train coach, both were deep in thought about their perplexing situation, and the train left the station without them being aware.

The train jerked to a halt, and both looked around. They realized it was their station and rushed to exit the coach. Once they'd descended the stairs from the overhead railway, they made their way back to the cruise ship. They passed through the customs shed and started to walk towards the gangway to board when a greeting came from above them.

They stopped and looked up and saw Vicki waving. They waved back, then both stopped, causing some who were following them to almost bump into them.

"That would be how he knows when we're leaving. He watches us leave the ship, then watches for us to come out from the secure area with our cases. He then tells his man on the ground that we're just coming out and describes us to them. He may even have mailed a photo of us, so they have a better idea of who to look out for. Once we get in the taxi, his man, the watcher, is able to tell the man on the motorbike the registration of the vehicle, and the tail is organised."

"But, Sheila, we still don't know how they find out when our next holiday is going to be."

"Agreed, but it's the last little obstacle to our solving the how of the burglaries."

They boarded the ship and went to their cabin. Once inside, both lay down on their beds and relaxed as the tiredness caused their eyes to close, and soon the only sound was the heavy breathing from two tired ladies taking a refreshing nap.

CHAPTER SEVENTEEN

October

The ladies woke with an announcement informing them that they were all on board and within the next hour, the ship would be on its way to their next port of call. They showered and changed into their evening dresses and made their way to the restaurant. Joining their usual table, they spoke to some of the ladies, asking if they had enjoyed Venice.

A few had been to Murano and had enjoyed the glass-blowing demonstration. They laughed as they told how they'd had a go and failed. Over the meal, talking was at a minimum, and once the meal was over, Sheila, Vicki, and Gill excused themselves to go up to the observation room again for dancing.

They settled in some seats, ordered a drink each, and waited for the hosts to arrive. Just five minutes later, the dance leaders and the hosts arrived and began to organise their seats, placing a glass of water for each one on the table. It wasn't long before the first dance was announced, and those ladies who wanted to dance waited expectantly to be asked.

Sheila was the first to be asked by the leader, Darren. He asked about her day and whether she'd enjoyed Venice. As she had expected, he was a lovely dancer. He returned her to her seat, and then Gloria announced the next dance.

Raymond asked Gill for that one, but still Gerald seemed to avoid asking either lady to dance with him. What was going on? They knew they would miss some, given that there were more ladies wanting to dance than hosts available.

A sequence dance was next called, and Gerald asked Gill for the dance. Sheila also got a chance to dance with Raymond, who preferred to be known as Ray apparently. The conversation was about the cruise and tours, or whether she'd wandered around Venice. He just asked general questions and nothing that could take her suspicions away from Gerald.

When the dance was over, Gill was escorted back to her place and with a nod to Sheila, Gerald walked back to the host's area to await the next dance. Vicki was asked to partner Ray on the next dance, and both Gill and Sheila missed out, but questions needed to be answered.

Gill turned to Sheila. "Nothing to report. Mundane comments about the heat, and did we get to St. Mark's Square? Coffee was mega expensive when he last went there. Not what I expected, but I did enjoy the dance."

"So he has either stepped back from our bait, or he has some other agenda. But what?"

The evening went on like this, and although both danced with their prime subject, neither had a single question relating to the watches or to where they lived. As the main hosts reminded them that there would be dancing tomorrow evening, Vicki excused herself again and rushed to the quiz, but Sheila and Gill planning to go to the evening show. They watched the three hosts leave the observation room and disappear to wherever they next went after this hour of dancing.

Making their way to the theatre, they noticed Mark and Gerald talking in front of them.

As they drew closer, Gerald said, "Ah, ladies, perhaps you can give us some advice. I've been on P&O lines, Saga, and with Fred Olsen, but we're at a loss as to what would be a good place to go to next. Mark and I don't like flying to the ship and then flying back, but you get to pick the interesting places to go to if you say you can do a particular cruise. Mark and I get on well with each other, but he doesn't want the bigger ships like P&O. Where are you considering going next, and with what cruise line?"

And there it was. A clever, innocent enough question that would elicit the information he required.

"Well, we want to go up to the Baltic Cities on a cruise next year," Gill said. "The annoyance is that it's from Dover."

Sheila looked at Gill, then said, "We want to book while we're on board, so we get the extra discount."

"Well, I'm sure you'll enjoy it. That sails towards the end of May, doesn't it?"

"Yes," said Sheila. "And it runs into June."

Gerald turned to Mark. "You see, Mark. The passengers always have a good idea of interesting places to visit. I've done this tour before and should be back in the Med at that time. You should book this, Mark. You'll enjoy it, and if the ladies book the cruise too, then you'll have two fine dancers to dance with. A bonus with this job, I must say."

"Okay, thank you, Gerald," said Mark, "and thank you too, ladies."

"Well, if you'll excuse me, ladies. I need to change my shirt. It was very hot up in the observation room, wasn't it?"

Not waiting for an answer, they both started to walk away.

"I think that's what is called a rhetorical question, don't you?"

Sheila watched the men walking away. "If you mean asking a question and not waiting to get an answer, then yes."

They made their way to the theatre and found two seats in an almost full house.

Settling back, they relaxed and watched the show, sipping their drinks as they enjoyed listening to the singer and her choice of music.

**

After breakfast the following morning, they returned to their cabin and decided to chat about their suspect and try to re-evaluate just what Gerald's information on them might be. He knew they had something of value to steal, and he knew that they were considering another cruise with Fred Olsen cruise lines, and that if they did, when and where it would go. He didn't have their addresses and hadn't asked. Would the gang wait seven months to rob them then? That seemed like an awfully long time to wait. When the cruise was over, the ladies decided they would observe vehicles—motorbikes, in particular—who looked as if they were following them.

With no accurate answers to their questions, they settled into a holiday mood for another two days at sea.

It was on the morning they arrived at Split in Croatia that news reached their ears about someone else having been burgled. Again, Vicki was the messenger. The couple had received a message from their daughter saying that she had contacted the police, and they had sealed the window that had been cut out. The man, Mr. Shellforth, had a collection of printer blocks, and they were all gone.

Other things had been taken, according to Vicki, who knew her from the bridge game they had been learning. Maureen Shellforth had said her chinaware, silver, and gold items had gone but that they weren't worth much and they had more sentimental value than anything.

Vicki said, "Poor things. It was their first time on a cruise, and it would be their last."

If this was their first time on a cruise, how could that have happened?

"Printers blocks? Whatever are they?" asked Gill.

"I asked the same question," said Vicki, "and Maureen said they were an old style of printing. They carved a picture into a block of wood, then when they printed using it, a picture was with the storyline in the paper. He also had etched copies that did the same thing, but the wooden ones were the most valuable."

"Well, well. Who would have thought that something like that could be worth stealing?" said Sheila.

"Anything that's a one-off becomes something of value. Look at postage stamps. In my youth, lots of people collected them, and when someone found one that had a fault on it, it became a rare thing, and vast amounts of money was offered for it. There's no accounting for what people will think of as collectable. It's only when someone else wants it, that it garners a market value. My neighbour's son collects wall tiles. I'm told that he thinks nothing of paying fifty pounds for one he hasn't got, and just because they're part of history."

"I've said it before: you have a mind of stored up, useless information until it's needed. Then suddenly, out of the atmosphere, you drag it up to let it see the light of day and let us bathe in the light of your wisdom."

Gill looked at Sheila. "What a long-winded compliment,

but I'll take it."

"Are you two okay? You aren't falling out with each other, are you?"

"No, we're always like this. Sheila plays the baddie, and of course, I'm the goodie!"

Sheila grinned. "Then we swap roles, but Gill just gets back into her normal character."

Both laughed, and Vicki shook her head, wondering what was going on. This was beyond her sense of humour. Nothing more happened, and the rest of the cruise passed without any other reports of thefts.

One little interesting comment from Vicki, after a dance with Mark, was that he'd asked if she knew whether Gill and Sheila had booked the Baltic Cities cruise yet. He had told him that she had no idea but to ask one of them. Vicki seemed to be a sensible woman, and she was direct with answers if she didn't like the questions.

On the day before they arrived back at Southampton, they booked the cruise, got their extra discount, and met Mark, who was helping a passenger sort out her disembarkation arrangements.

"Just booked the next cruise?" he asked.

Sheila said that they had. She knew now that Gerald used others who unwillingly helped him find answers and now, apart from their address, he had everything he needed. Although this wasn't factual, now they had a format that would stand up as the means and way of stealing from passengers if the police were interested. But tomorrow, when they disembarked, it would be interesting to see if they could spot anyone following them.

Mark wished them a safe journey home tomorrow and told them that he looked forward to seeing them on the cruise next year. They returned to their cabin, put the paperwork into the safe, and went to see what entertainment there was prior to the last evening dinner. They end the day with a show.

***

It was a dull and overcast morning that greeted them as they drew back the curtains in their cabin. It was all a rush; they were required to vacate their cabin by nine thirty. So it was a quick swill, dress, and dash to the restaurant to have a quick breakfast. Then they went back to the cabin to collect their hand luggage before going to wait for their cabin numbers to be called.

The big cases had been put outside the cabin door before they'd retired to bed, and during the night, a crew member had collected them and taken them down to the hold, ready to be transported to the sheds that they went through when they arrived.

Once the cabin numbers were called, all done by colours, everyone with that colour code was invited to disembark. When their colour code was called, Gill and Sheila said their goodbyes and walked downstairs to the lower deck and out into the sunshine. Well, no, not quite. It was overcast, but the sun was bravely trying to push through the stubborn clouds, which, with persistent determination, kept covering the sun's face.

Gill looked up. "England never disappoints for weather, does it?"

"Not often," said Sheila as she searched for their two cases in the shed.

Finding Gill's, she returned to look for hers, then once retrieved, they stacked the hand luggage on top of the cases and headed out to the taxi rank. The drivers were lined up with names on their cards. The ladies walked slowly along the ranks, looking for their own.

Sheila paused and looked back at the ship, and there on the top deck looking over the side, was Gerald talking into his phone. She looked around to see if any of the drivers had a phone to their ear, but that was useless. Lots were wearing those hands-free earphones, so she would get no luck there.

"Sheila, that driver is ours, see? Blakeney and Chancel."

Sheila pulled her case to the waiting taxi, glanced back to the ship, and saw Gerald close his phone and walk away as she passed her case to the driver. They got in and once the driver had checked with them their addresses, he put his sat nav on, and they started on their journey home.

Now came the problem of looking out of the back window to see if they were being followed. Sheila had an idea. She put her finger to her lips as a sign for silence to Gill. "Driver, I'm writing a book, and I want to see how hard it would be to spot someone following us. Would you mind if I used my face mirror and kept looking to see if I could do this? Only my detective needs to find out if someone is following him."

"I don't mind at all, lady, but if it were me wanting to follow this cab, then it would be that motorbike a few cars back. Put in your writing that you found it suspicious that a high-powered motorbike made no effort to overtake my taxi when he had a reasonably clear road in front of him."

"Oh, yes, I see him behind the blue car."

"That's right, lady, and I noticed them because I ride one myself. That's a Kawasaki Ninja 400 in yellow, just like mine."

The driver left the ladies to watch the motorcycle until the driver indicated he was turning off the main road and taking a lesser road towards the outskirts of Andover and the route to their homes.

Sheila adjusted her mirror and watched to see if the motorbike followed, but she couldn't see it.

"The rider has pulled up behind the black car at the junction we just took," said the taxi driver. "This research has got me going. I keep glancing into my mirror to see if I can see the splash of yellow."

"Well, as he's clearly not following us but gave us a subject to use to test if it could be done, I think I'll say that part in my book is a big yes."

The taxi driver glanced into his mirror. "Hold your horses. He's overtaking a few cars behind us and getting closer."

Sheila resisted using her mirror. "As long as you aren't risking your safety, would you let us know if he follows us on any other turns as we near our homes?"

"No, lady, it's fine by me. It's usually a boring journey, but you two have made it more interesting, and I have to use my rear-view mirror, so it's no problem."

They travelled on towards Andover and eventually the driver turned into Gill's cul-de-sac. "Your yellow motorbike rider has gone on." He turned at the bottom of the road and drove back up to Gill's house.

Gill got out, and he retrieved her luggage from the book. She looked up the road and saw a motorcycle helmet poking around the corner, but he quickly pulled back as if he'd seen her watching for him.

She leaned into the car. "I just glanced up the road, and I'm pretty sure I saw the motorbike rider poking his head around the end of the road. This is exciting, isn't it? Give me a ring once you're back. Bye."

Sheila nodded. "I'll let you know if I see him again. See you soon."

Gill shut the car door and walked to her front door where the taxi driver had put the big case and stood waiting.

"Do you need a hand in with the case? It's a bit heavy."

"Thank you, yes, please." Gill opened the door and held it wide so that the driver could place the case at the end of the staircase. She gave him a tip. "Thank you again."

When the driver got back in the taxi, Sheila sat back for the ten minutes or so journey to her home. Although it was lovely to get away, it was always great to be home—unless, of course, you arrived home to find that unscrupulous and unwelcome visitors had been in while you were away.

Her thoughts were interrupted by the driver. "Are you sure you didn't hire someone to shadow you home for your book writing? Because the yellow Kawasaki is behind me again."

"No, I really didn't. But it is strange that he's come the same way as us."

He turned into Sheila's road and pulled up outside. He got out and opened the door for her. She positioned herself to look at the driver as he pulled her case from the boot but also, without being too obvious, made it so that she could look up the road at the same time.

Yes! There was someone at the corner, and she thought she could see him scribbling something on a pad of notebook.

"Can I take this in for you, love?" he asked when they were at the door with her luggage.

"That would be very kind, thank you," she said and tipped him.

"Quite an exciting ride, that," he said. "If you ever need another ride to the port, then I'd be very willing. You have my card. Let me know when you've finished your book, and I'll get a signed copy."

She tapped his card with her fingernail. "Absolutely," she said, though she had no idea at all how she was supposed to write the book *and* catch the bag guys. Maybe she would put pen to paper when all this was finished.

Sheila went upstairs to the front bedroom and looked up the road to the junction. She waited for ten to fifteen minutes and was about to give up when a man in a long brown coat and a trilby came around the corner. He crossed to her side of the road and walked down towards her home. He seemed to be checking the house at the top of the road and as he approached her house, he kept glancing at the other houses.

He paused briefly outside her home, then continued on. A few doors down, he stopped and took out a pen and notepad, then scribbled something down, presumably her house number. After that, he crossed the road and returned the way he'd come.

A few minutes later, she saw a yellow motorbike go past the junction in the direction of Gill's house. Sheila took out her mobile phone. "Hi, it's me. Get up into your front bedroom and keep an eye out at the top of your road. The motorbike rider has just been down to my house, and I'm sure he took my address. Expect him anytime soon. He's disguised himself in a trilby and a long brown coat. Let me know once you get a visit."

Sure enough, after ten minutes had passed, a man fitting Sheila's description came around the corner, crossed to Gill's side of the road, and took her number down. Not long after, she saw the flash of yellow as the rider sped past the end of her road.

"Well?" asked Sheila when Gill called.

"Yes, I am as you ask. I've just come back from a holiday with some woman who wanted me to stand at my window on my bad leg, watching for strange men to pass my home."

"Gill, forget your leg. Did he come to you or not?"

"Yes, just like you said he would. And he took my house

number too."

"So, our suspect has all the information he needs to drop into your home and lift the watches he thinks are there. Now it's time for another visit to the police to go over what we've discovered."

"But the criminals won't visit us until next year. It's always when people leave to go on a cruise, so we don't have any worries until then. Other poor people will, of course, because they aren't going to stop until we make them."

"No, we don't. But another visit to the police is now a must. Sleep well, and I'll see you soon."

"I shall be pleased to get a good night's sleep, but all this cold, damp weather is playing havoc with my bad leg."

"Mm, nothing to do with the thought of a dance with Arthur Walters?"

"Perish the thought. Good night."

"Night."

And they hung up.

As Sheila walked back to her suitcase to unpack it, she let her mind drift to the bait and the fish they seemed to have on the end of the line. *I wonder if it's enough to get the police frothing at the mouth.*

CHAPTER EIGHTEEN

November

The trees had all but lost their leaves, and with the cold winds from the north, the few that remained would soon join the rest at the base of their creators to rot and become nutrients for next year's new growth.

Sheila had rung the police at Southampton once again, and this time she got a far more favourable reception from them. They'd been home for just over a week and were bemoaning the change in temperature.

They'd decided to ring once the forecast was going to be dry, and after almost a week of rain and blustery showers, they welcomed the prospect of going out into the sunshine, although it wasn't anywhere near as hot as they'd been used to.

Once again, Sheila picked up Gill, and they drove down to Southampton, following the old route that took them into the car park across from the police station.

The difference on this visit was that they had no set time to arrive. They'd been told they would be welcome at any time in the morning, and that D.I. Wainwright would receive them immediately.

Gill looked at the plastic seats in the reception, not looking forward to sitting on them at all, but once they'd given their names, the police sergeant said, "This young constable will take you both upstairs. The inspector is expecting you."

Gill looked at Sheila and raised an eyebrow. "What's going on?" she whispered.

Sheila shrugged.

The constable took them upstairs and the inspector himself came to the door and welcomed them. "Ladies, welcome. It's really nice to see you both again." He ushered them in. "Sandra, would you take their coats, please? You remember Sandra, my constable, who was with us when you last came to visit."

"Yes," they replied as Sandra took their coats and hung them up.

"Can I offer you tea or coffee? We can do better than the machine stuff you usually get at a police station. I have my own machine, and it makes a really good brew," he said. "But Sandra is a dab hand at getting a good strong cup of tea from a tea bag if that's what you'd prefer."

"Tea for me, please," said Sheila, and Gill asked for the same.

Wainwright leaned forward on his desk. "Well, while Sandra sorts the drinks out, can I ask if you're here to offer a follow-up on your last visit about the burglaries? Or is this something new?"

Sheila looked at Gill, who could hardly contain herself. The change in the way they were being received was remarkable, almost as if they were royalty.

"Inspector," said Gill, "do you remember when we last came to you and put forward our theory about the boss member of the gang co-ordinating the robberies from a cruise ship? You seemed to think that we were wasting your time, yet now, you're all sweetness and light. Do we take it that the police have investigated our perception of the way the thefts are organised and that you now concur with our thoughts?"

D.I. Wainwright sat back in his chair, causing it to groan as it took his weight. "Well, that was straight to the jugular…" he looked down at his note in front of him, "Gill."

"I don't want to waste police time, so please answer my question. Your answer will decide if we want to impart any further information."

D.I. Wainwright looked at Sheila, and she nodded. Gill was letting him know in no uncertain terms that she wasn't impressed last time, and no number of cups of tea or coffee would do this time.

"Okay, Gill and, um," he glanced at his note, "Shirley—"

"Sheila," she said.

"What? Oh, sorry about that; I can't even read my own writing. I'd like to bring you up to date with our investigations and also to thank you for bringing that information to our attention. After you left, I felt it would be useful to check a few other cases that we had on our books. We found thefts you didn't know about that had similar links to your thefts."

Gill and Sheila looked at each other. "So you did follow up on our theory," Gill said, and you found more cases that were—how did you term it? Oh, yes, circumstantial evidence."

D.I. Wainwright sighed. "I hold my hands up and admit it. If you hadn't come into this station and given me your theory, we wouldn't have found this link. But it's led us to make a connection with the southeast division District Inspector. He's also been digging into his past cases and found ones not on your list. In fact, he found quite a lot which occurred whilst the victims were on a cruise."

"So it's been going on for some time?" Sheila asked.

"Yes, it certainly seems that way. We also checked up on your suspect, and though he wasn't on some of the cruise ships when it happened, he'd been on one with the victims sometime before, as you both suspected."

"Well, I can't believe it. You're actually saying we got it right."

"Yes, Gill," he replied and smirked as he glanced at his note, which confirmed he had it right this time. "Unfortunately, the fact remains that we can't prove it."

"That fact does remain, however, *we* have some more information that might help you." Sheila took a mouthful of her tea, now just at the perfect temperature. "After we visited you, we hatched a plan to see if our suspect, and you'll note, inspector, that I still say suspect, would take some bait we might dangle in front of his nose."

"But I told you not to do that. You need to leave the crook-chasing to us."

"Yes, but as you gave us the distinct impression that you'd paid no attention to our theory, we decided to see if we could stimulate our suspect's interest, especially if he thought one of us had something of value or interest to his gang. We thought that would get his attention, you see, so we fabricated a valuable collection of watches left by Gill's husband and let him accidentally find out about it."

"Goodness, you both took an extraordinary risk."

Wainwright licked his lips though, unable to contain his glee. "Did he show any interest?"

"Oh yes," said Gill. "We let it be known that the collection had an Omega underwater watch in the collection, and he had a gleam in his eye when he overheard that."

"Did he ask any questions about the collection at any other time?"

"No, but he had advance knowledge that we lived near Southampton and that Gill's husband owned a worthwhile collection with a rather large value. He also knew we were going on another cruise next year, and now he's got our addresses, he's all set to send in his team when we leave. You see, once they have all those details, it doesn't matter if the victims don't travel for six months. They have a list of people who are of interest, and they can just wait until the date of sailing comes. Then, we expect that they decide on a night for the break-in, and it's over and done with. If they find any other things of interest, then that's a bonus."

Wainwright leaned back in his suffering chair and swivelled towards Sandra, who had been recording the conversation. "Sandra, to hell with my diet, break out that box of biscuits, please. I think I need something sweet. These lovely ladies have placed even more worthwhile information into our laps."

His chair gave a groan as if protesting against the extra weight it was likely to have to bear. Wainwright stopped swivelling as the tin of biscuits came, and he sat forward to open it. Sheila and Gill took one each. "Help yourself, Sandra, while I go over this information."

He dipped his chocolate digestive into his drink then took a mouthful. After he'd swallowed, he said, "Something that I haven't grasped is how he found out your address."

Gill wiggled her eyebrows. "He got someone to follow us home."

D.I. Wainwright almost dropped his remaining bit of the biscuit. "He arranged for someone to follow you? How do you know that?"

Sheila relayed the events of their return journey, replete with the yellow motorbike and the odd chap in his long coat and trilby.

D.I. Wainwright took another biscuit and chewed on it as he again sank back into his chair to contemplate this new information. "The crafty B. Sorry, ladies, but the audacity of it staggers me. It's so well planned." He shook his head and sighed deeply. "So, in essence, you've set your homes up for a visit by ruffians who don't care about people or property *and* risked a possible confrontation with them. You know that they could cause one or both of you to end up in hospital. This is not good, ladies, not good at all."

"I don't think so, inspector. They take what they want and don't make a mess. That's a careful sort of criminal. If they are going to visit our home, it'll be when we have our next holiday and not at any other time. Time is on their side, so they don't need to chance breaking in while we're out shopping or some such thing. They know we're going on a cruise, so they know the house is empty and when we're going to return."

"Yes, I understand. Nonetheless, you've put yourselves in danger."

"To a small degree, yes," said Gill, "but that's a risk we wanted to take to help you catch these people and put them behind bars."

He munched on another biscuit as he ruminated some more. After a few moments of silence, he said, "You said the bike was a yellow Kawasaki. Did the rider pull up alongside your taxi, for you to see the make of the bike? Please be factual, because it's a very important point."

"We found out that our taxi driver has an identical bike," Sheila said. "He has a Kawasaki Ninja 400, and when you catch these people, I bet you'll find that they have the same model."

"That's very precise. But if you're right, it's very important information." He took another biscuit and chewed on it as his chair groaned once again. Finally, he sat forward. "Look, ladies, I can't say I'm happy about you putting yourselves in harm's way, but I *am* very grateful for all that you've done to help solve this catalogue of thefts along the south coast." He smiled at them both. "I'd like you to tell me the dates of your cruise next year. When you leave for your cruise, we'll have someone watch your house, Gill. They seem to pick the third or fourth evening, but we'll cover them all, just in case. When they come, as I'm sure you're going to be proved right, then we should bag the lot of them."

"What about the leader?" asked Sheila. "If you think you're going to catch him, you might be out of luck if he's on the boat with us. He could hear that the gang have been arrested, step off at the next port and vanish."

"Who's going to tell him?"

"That's the point, isn't it," said Gill. "You don't know their system. You don't know whether they send a coded message to him, or even call him. If he doesn't get the message, he'll know something has gone wrong. Why would he wait to see? Far better to take on a new persona and start all over again with a new gang, or something entirely new. This man is not a common criminal. He's intelligent and a planner. For him, the others can take the fall for everything, and he gets away with it clean."

D.I. Wainwright rested his arms on the desk and clasped his hands together. "It's a pity I didn't have you two on my team years ago. If I could, I'd offer you both a job here and now. Regretfully, I can't, but," he paused and selected his wording carefully, "excuse me for saying this, for ladies of a more mature age, you've both got very agile minds."

Gill looked at Sheila and then at the inspector. "Well, thank you for that. It makes us feel much better about the whole thing." She passed a piece of paper to the inspector. "I've put the dates of our cruise next year on this slip of paper, as you requested."

"Thank you for that. We'll file this in our very bulky folder, thanks to both of your efforts." He stood and nodded to Sandra, indicating the end of the meeting, "Well, ladies, you're going to have to leave all the other cases with us, but please contact me nearer the date you sail next year. In the meantime, I'll liaise with the inspector for the southeast end of the area that the gang have been busy in and inform him of the events going on here."

He stood and shook hands with them both. "I can't thank

you enough for your cooperation on this. Stay in touch. If we catch them in the interim period, I'll be sure to let you know."

The ladies took their coats from Sandra and pulled them on ready for the cold wind that had blasted them as they came from the car park.

"I'll take you downstairs and see you out," Sandra said. "Please take care crossing the road, it's very busy again."

At the exit, she shook both of their hands and closed the door after they left. Gill and Sheila quickly made their way to the carpark.

Once in the car, Sheila sat for a moment. "I don't know about you, but I could use a good drink."

"Get me home, and I'll join you."

Sheila eased out of the car park. A G&T would go down very well once they got home. She certainly felt that they'd earned one.

CHAPTER NINETEEN

January to June

With Christmas and the New Year celebrations behind them, winter began to release its grip and the first snowdrops lifted their heads. The countdown started for the ladies' future holiday, both having avoided the COVID variant that seemed to be taking everyone by surprise. The government hadn't stopped parties but had asked everyone to be aware of this new variant. The result was that both struggled with their decision to go or not to go to their club's New Year party dance.

In the end, they went, and although it was a very depleted showing, they did accept a good number of dances on the evening. Once Gill saw that Arthur Walters was nowhere to be seen, her leg got miraculously better, and to added to the fun, a new male dancer called Barry had joined the club, and he whisked them around the floor to lovely music.

When they left the party, after staying to clear up with the other committee members, Gill declared that that had been the best New Year's dance the club had put on so far.

The chilled north wind swept in with February, and flurries of snow also blew in. Dancing was cancelled for the month due to the hall having a heating problem, so the ladies met up for a chat in each other's homes just to maintain contact. Inevitably, the conversation always drifted to their upcoming holiday and the possible arrest of the gang when they tried to rob Gill's home.

Of course, it wasn't her real home, but although she was now living in her new home, she'd decided not to sell the old house so that when the police caught the criminals, she would rent it out instead. That way, there was no rush for her to remove some of the odd bits of furniture that she'd not made up her mind about whether to keep or not. There were curtains at the windows and from the outside, it looked as if it someone still lived there.

They hadn't seen the yellow motorbike come near either of their homes and had reassured D.I. Wainwright that they were both okay. He'd even sent them a Christmas card with the message, *To my super granny sleuths*.

By mid-February, snow had fallen and settled in a surprise storm that hadn't been forecast. As usual, when a layer of snow welcomed the workers, chaos reigned. The council blamed the forecasters, who'd said there would be only a slight chance of snow. Unfortunately, they hadn't anticipated the amount that came.

By the end of the week, it was mostly gone, and normality returned.

February gave a sigh as March came in with strong winds and pouring rain. It was relentless, and reports of flooding and trees falling down disrupted power lines and driving conditions. Both of the intrepid ladies stayed in, warm near the fire.

But like all things, the gale passed on across the Channel and the news reported that the Dutch were pumping water from the dikes into the sea to avoid flooding over there.

April arrived quietly and brought slight clouds and welcome sunshine, and the meetings for the ladies' clubs began to attract a few new members.

A visit to Gills home by D.I. Wainwright and Sandra surprised them, but once he was comfortable in an armchair that didn't complain at his bulk, he said, "Thank you for letting me make this call to your home." He looked at Sheila. "And thank you for agreeing to meet here at such short notice. There are a few things that need to be said before the final steps are taken to implement your plan. First, I must tell you that the gang are once again very active, and therefore I must give you the chance to opt out of this."

Sheila looked at Gill, who shook her head. "We're not interested in backing out now, of course. We haven't come this far and put in so much work to be scared off now. Let's be clear, inspector, we'll have more danger of falling off the cruise ship. We won't be here when they visit; your people will be the ones in danger. Added to this, the architect of this scheme won't be on our cruise ship. He will be on a

Saga ship, and we'll be on a Fred Olen cruise. How could he threaten us?"

They were committed to seeing this through and putting the gang behind bars, where they belonged.

D.I. Wainwright stood up and picked up his hat. "Thank you, ladies. May I wish you both a very good holiday. Come back safely, and I hope to have good news for you both on your return. Two of my team will be back about a week before you leave to fit the things they discussed. They will contact you," he said to Gill, "to let you know when."

It was a happier detective that left the ladies.

"I don't know about you, but I could do with a stiff drink," said Gill as she closed the door. This visit reminded them that the months were marching on, and the holiday was not so far away.

April showers came and went as the ladies went on with their lives—the highlight of which was Gill dancing with Arthur Walters. When he escorted her back to the table, it was as if he'd gained a new lease of life.

Sheila couldn't stop herself and had to comment. "I see your bad leg has got better again, so much so that you couldn't say no to your most ardent admirer."

"Well, yes. It had become difficult now that I'm having so many dances with Barry. And, yes, my bad leg has improved since you so caringly ask, so I danced with Arthur Walters… Well, I walked with him." Gill giggled and sipped her tea.

"I do hope you aren't going to monopolise Barry's time on the dance floor, especially now Arthur is in the frame."

"Meow. Fur bristling, is it?"

Sheila laughed, and Gill joined in. They lifted their drink and drank a silent toast.

May seemed in a hurry to reach the end of its time and hand over to June. So many things had to be done as Gill finally sorted out her new house and discarded all the things she didn't want. Sheila helped arrange the lounge and dining room to make it look as if she still lived there. The police came and did their thing for the security, fitting an alarm and a few cameras, all linked to a box in the hallway. They also called down to Sheila's home and put in a few cameras, just in case.

As the last two weeks of May came, the countdown started for their cruise. The taxi was booked, and most of the things they required on board were organised and laid out ready to go into the case. The hardest thing for both of them was sorting their clothes out. What would go with what. Which shoes would complement this or that? It took almost half a day…and was amended the next day…and adjusted the following day.

They packed on the evening before they travelled to Dover to join the cruise ship.

Gill rang Sheila that evening, and said, "No panic. I just wanted to check that the taxi driver has confirmed the pickup tomorrow morning."

Sheila confirmed that the driver would pick her up first, then call on Gill. "Then it's that long journey to Dover," Gill said. "I really hate that."

"Yes, it's not the best of options, but at least we don't have to go all the way up to Liverpool."

"Well, we're all set," said Gill. "Let the adventure begin. Night then. See you in the morning."

As Sheila hung up, she had to wipe her nose again. What an inopportune time to get a cold.

The morning came and their friendly taxi driver came for Sheila on time. Sheila wasn't feeling quite as well as she ought to be, but could one get flu towards the end of May? He loaded her luggage, and once she was ready, he headed to Gill's house.

Gill was waiting—and so was someone else. At the top of the cul-de-sac, a familiar yellow motorbike idled quietly. Once Gill's cases were packed, the driver started on his way. Following behind was the yellow peril, four or five cars back.

They stopped for a comfort break but could see nothing of the yellow bike as they got out and stretched their legs. Returning after making use of the facilities, they stood near the taxi. Not wanting to make it obvious they were looking, they faced each other as if they were talking, but instead, they looked around for the bike.

"Well, I don't see the driver of the motorbike. I wonder if

he decided we're on our way and gone home?"

Gill simply shrugged, and when the driver returned, they were soon back on the road towards Dover. When they arrived at the port, the driver stopped at the sign for to drop the ladies' suitcases, then they moved on to the embarkation shed, and the taxi driver stopped to retrieve their hand luggage from the boot.

Sheila pulled out an envelope from inside her jacket. "Cash as you requested, plus a little extra. Thank you very much. I'll message you with a return timing the day before we return in case the ship gets held up."

With a promise that he would be waiting on their return, he got back in the taxi and drove back out the way he had come in.

As they went to go into the shed to check in, Gill noticed the yellow motorbike in the car park directly opposite them. The rider was watching them. "Don't look now, but our shadow is parked directly across from here watching us."

Sheila, who'd been busy blowing her nose, said, "So, he just drove here in front of us, but he did know where we were going."

They both picked up their hand luggage and headed to the check-in area.

Except they couldn't get there…

In front of them was a group of people asking them questions. When Gill and Sheila got to the front of the queue, a lady asked them both, "In the last four or five days, have you or any other member of your family suffered from flu-like symptoms?"

Sheila sniffed. "Well, I do have a slight cold now, but I'm taking paracetamol to help break it."

"As you've confirmed you do have a cold," the lady said, "please step into the big red area over there and sit on one of the chairs. Someone will be with you shortly to do a check on you. As you came together, please join your friend," she said to Gill.

They sat for a short while before another lady arrived. She was dressed in a white coat and trousers and wore a mask over her head with clear plastic for her to look through.

She asked them to confirm their names and that they had travelled together. After confirming this, they were then asked to follow her to an area where they would both be tested for the COVID virus. Gill and Sheila sat in a cubicle each with a person in a space suit who sorted out a swab and other things they would need.

"Just relax. This won't take long," They pushed swabs up their noses and once satisfied, took the swabs away for analysis.

Ten minutes later, the lady came back. "I'm very sorry, but we can't let you board." She pointed to Sheila. "You have COVID. You should go home, take paracetamol to help your body resist it, and above all, rest." She turned to Gill. "You don't have it, but I'm afraid the same applies to you. You've been in contact with this lady for quite some time, so with regret, you can't board the ship."

Sheila was almost in tears when they were asked what the cabin number was so that they could retrieve their cases. They sat waiting in a yellow area, an ironic colour thought Gill. After half an hour had passed, their cases arrived.

"We've arranged for a taxi to take you home, at your expense, of course, and the driver is aware that one of you has COVID. The front of the car is blocked off by a thick plastic screen, and he'll have his windows open on the journey. He'll need you to pay by card, not cash, thus reducing contact with you."

"This is awful," said Gill. "My friend is being made to feel like a person affected with leprosy. We've both had our vaccinations, as I expect so have most of the people boarding."

"I'm sorry, but with this new variant and the government restrictions, we have no choice but to decline your boarding." She held out a letter. "You will need this letter to claim your money back on your insurance. Fred Olsen cruise line can't make a refund direct for complying with government rulings." She passed another copy to Gill.

A man came through the door and called out, "Chancel and Blakeney," and the lady waved to him.

He wiped the handles of the cases with an antiseptic cloth.

"This way, please, ladies," he said and walked away, clearly expecting them to trail along behind.

They picked up their hand luggage and followed him to his taxi, aware that others in the line behind them had seen them pulled out and were now being escorted from the building. Sheila lagged behind her friend, both numb with shock. They stopped by the taxi and as they waited for the driver to load the cases, Sheila burst into tears. "Gill, I am so sorry about this. I have no idea how I caught COVID, but I promise you, I'll make it up to you." Sheila was racked with guilt that she'd ruined their long-awaited holiday—and their plans to finally get that gang of thieves arrested.

The journey back felt interminably long, but eventually, the driver pulled into Gill's road. As he unloaded her cases, Sheila said "I'll clear the taxi bill once we get to my house. You just take some paracetamol in case you've picked this virus up."

The driver didn't offer to take the case to the door. He simply turned, got in the taxi, and drove away.

On arriving at Sheila's house, the driver again took out the case, placed it on the path. He looked at his meter and told her the charge for driving to both houses and going back. "As you're paying by card, hang on a minute while I pick up a signal."

Sheila was shocked at the price. "I shall need a receipt, please, to send to the insurance company." She made sure she pressed no to the question on the machine about would she like to include a tip or not. Once he was satisfied, she put in her pin, and he gave her a receipt.

Sheila trudged down the path, as the driver drove away. At her front door, she unlocked it and lugged the case into the hall. She locked the door behind her and burst into tears. *Why, oh why did this happen now. Why couldn't it have been a few weeks before.* When she'd gathered herself, she turned the alarm off that the police had set up. She then went into the kitchen, made a cup of Ovaltine, and took two paracetamol. She sighed deeply at the sight of her luggage at the bottom of the stairs and swallowed down another burst of tears. She decided to face it tomorrow and went up to her bedroom.

It was four o'clock in the afternoon when she climbed into the bed. She pulled the covers over her and broke down again, sobbing uncontrollably.

If Gill picks this up from me, I will never forgive myself. What did I do to deserve this?

CHAPTER TWENTY

June

The following morning, Sheila lay in bed, thinking things over. There was so much to do now. Once she'd decided she would have some toast and marmalade for breakfast, she slipped out of bed. Her head pounded like someone was playing a set of drums inside it. She slowed her pace in case moving fast meant they played louder.

It didn't help every time she blew her nose, but better that than letting it dribble down all over her top.

She had her breakfast and took more tablets in an effort to ease the headache down to a bearable level. Sheila, then looked at the case, waiting to be unpacked. Not today, she thought. Today was not going to be good.

The ringing of the telephone caused the drummer to step up the beat.

"Hello," Sheila said quietly.

"Goodness, you do sound rough. Anything I can do to help?"

"Well, you can speak quieter. I have a percussion band going on in my head."

"I think you should take some more pain killers," Gill said softly, "and get back to bed. I had a phone call from the inspector asking why they came back yesterday. I explained what had happened, and he said at this late juncture, he wouldn't call his team in from watching my old home. There was still a remote possibility that the gang hadn't been informed. He added that he hoped we'd both come through this with no problems."

After their conversation ended, Sheila spent the day asleep in her chair or just mooched around the house until it came to her bedtime. The continued tablets seemed to help dull the drummer, who had softened to a thump in her brain.

She went upstairs and having not bothered to dress, took her dressing gown off and climbed into bed. She didn't remember much after that. She just allowed the blackness to sweep over her, and soon she was asleep.

The next morning, she felt a little better. By lunchtime, she'd almost finished unpacking the case, and that gave her a slight lift.

The phone call from Gill gave her another boost.

"Hello, Sheila. You sound a little better, but how's the drum kit going?"

"I think I've managed to evict the players. I'm muzzy headed but feeling better. I even unpacked my suitcase."

"Now that is good news, and here's some more; I did a COVID test this morning and got a negative result. I won't be visiting, however, unless you need some food, then I'll get it for you."

"Thank you, Gill, but I'll cope for the short time this is going to be. Good news about you so far avoiding it." Sheila ended the call and sank into her chair thinking how fortunate she was to have such a good friend. After a little sleep, Sheila watched a film in the afternoon, and by the evening, the drummer in her head had started once again. She was sweaty and hot and cold in waves, so she took two more tablets to help. At nine thirty, she dragged herself up to her bedroom, undressed, and climbed into her bed. Once again, she drifted off to sleep in a very short while.

***

Robert's next nocturnal visit was booked in, and Gerald had called to tell him that the two ladies had sailed.

Though still unsettled about Gerald lies, Robert had decided to go on with the arrangement until it suited him to stop it. John had watched the two ladies being picked up from their homes, and he'd come back to report that they'd gone into the boarding shed after their cases had been sent on a conveyer to the ship.

Tonight was the night to claim a lovely collection of watches, owned by one of the ladies.

Unfortunately, John—the daft bugger—had somehow managed to mix up which old woman lived in which house.

It was the first time that he'd had to follow two people to two different houses, and it had gone wrong. Without sending photos of the two women, Robert supposed the mix up was of his own doing. Nevertheless, he hadn't informed Gerald of the little mess. They had both addresses so they would visit both houses.

Their unwitting clients had been at sea for two days now, so it was time to make the visit. Robert smiled at the use of the word time. Quite appropriate, he thought. At midnight, with the gang all assembled, they set off along the south coast in the lorry towards Southampton and then followed the sat nav to the first address.

It wasn't a very pleasant night, squally showers and strong gusts of wind made their journey a hard task, but eventually, they arrived and parked outside. They made their way down the drive and around to the back of the house.

John had the glass cutters and sucker pads at the ready. He cut the pane of glass out, removed it, and placed it carefully on the lawn. Badger lifted John through the window, and moments later, he unlatched the back door. Billy went into the hall to see if any alarm systems were on but found one and it wasn't turned on. The house also had cameras, but Billy wasn't worried since he was wearing a balaclava mask over his face, so any film taken before he cut the power to the cameras would be useless. His little box that he scanned around each room soon caused the recordings to freeze.

He returned to the back door and opened it to let everyone move in. Then he went into the hallway and took the front door off the latch in case they needed to get out fast.

"Take that mask off now you've sorted the security side of things and help us," Robert said. "Search one of the bedrooms for anything that might look valuable. If you're not sure, bring it to me, then go and find something else. The more you find, the more everyone's share will be."

"No problem, boss." Billy followed John, who pointed to one bedroom before going into another.

Not wishing to let them down, Billy went into the room and shone his small torch around the space, making sure that he kept the light away from the window. He saw a small cabinet by the bed with a statue on it. He picked up the figure and examined it.

It was a solid bronze sculpture of a half man, half horse. He went around to the other side of the bed to find another sculpture of a half *woman*, half horse.

"A pair," he said out loud.

Then Sheila woke and sat up abruptly. "Who on earth are you? And what on earth are you doing in my bedroom?"

More from reflex than forethought, Billy struck Sheila on the side of her head with the statue. As she slumped sideways, he dropped the sculptures and ran out of the bedroom.

He rushed downstairs and grabbed Robert's shoulders. "There was a woman up there asleep, but she woke up and spoke to me. I didn't reply, gov. I just knocked her out and came straight down here to you."

"Oh God, we don't need that."

"Badger!" Robert shouted. "I'm going upstairs to see what the hell is going on. Young Billy has hit a woman and knocked her out, so gather what we've got, bag it, and get John ready to go as soon as I return." He took Billy by the arm and pulled him upstairs. "Which room were you in, Billy?"

"This one here," said Billy, looking very worried.

Robert moved over to the side of the double bed where he could see the shape of a body. He looked at the woman and then at Billy. He shook his head and lifted her arm, feeling for a pulse.

Nothing. Nothing but lots of blood.

"What did you hit her with, Billy?"

"A brass statue," he said and picked it up from the floor.

"We need to get out of here pretty damn quick, because you've killed her."

Still clutching the statue covered in blood at its base, Billy picked up the other one. They moved swiftly downstairs, where Badger and John waited for them, both looking very anxious.

"Billy's done for her," Robert said. "He hit her with a brass statue. Let's get out of here. Make sure we leave nothing behind and try not to make another sound."

They bagged up the few items they'd managed to find, put the two statues in a separate bag, and left via the back door. Once they were all back in the lorry, they set off back to base.

But it was a sad journey home; this was the last thing Robert wanted to happen. The old girl didn't deserve to die, but now the whole game had changed. This was murder, and there was no way around it. The more Robert thought about it, the more his hands shook. Fear had all sorts of strange effects on people, and on Robert, it was his urinary tract.

"Pull over at the next layby, Badger. I need to water a bush."

After Robert had made himself comfortable, they continued on their way. Usually Badger and John would leave Robert at his place and return home in the lorry after dropping him off, but Robert wanted to have a word with them before they went.

"Right, lads," said Robert. "Return home as normal. Say nothing and do nothing. We wore gloves, so no one can prove anything." He focused on Billy. "I know you were scared, and you didn't mean to kill that woman, but you did. If you say anything, anything at all, someone may overhear you, and you'll end up doing a long stretch in prison as someone's girlfriend."

Robert turned to Badger and John. "A lot is riding on silence—everyone's silence. Keep an eye on each other. I'll keep an eye on the local newspapers to see when it's reported and what the police think they know. Meantime, we stick to our legitimate work. Badger, I need you for a special removal job tomorrow. I should have it sorted by lunchtime."

"Okay, boss. Leave it to us to sort out Billy."

They left to go home, and Robert trudged upstairs to his home, which didn't look so welcoming now as it once had.

***

The following morning, Robert peered into the mirror and looked at the bags under his eyes through lack of sleep. He shook his head and went to make a cup of tea, into which he poured a small slug of whisky. *Medicinal purposes,* he thought.

He slumped into an armchair, looking at nothing in particular, his mind replaying the view of the dead woman. The amount of blood around her head had surprised him, and his hands had been shaking when he lifted her hand to feel for a pulse. Handling a corpse… How the hell had it come to this? His stomach heaved and, knowing what was coming, he ran to the bathroom to be violently sick.

Once he'd done, he flushed the toilet and returned to his chair, not bothering with the rest of his laced tea.

Robert sat a while, then got up from the chair and walked around the room, moving this way or that, doing nothing. He wanted more than anything to get his mind off the mess they were in.

Finally, at ten o'clock, he rang Gerald and while waiting for him to pick up, paced around the room. "I have some important news for you about our work yesterday. Are you free to talk?"

"Yes, I'm in my cabin, and I'm alone. What's up?"

"We made the visit as scheduled last night, but unfortunately, the owner was still in the house."

"What? I'm astonished. I thought you said that John had checked all was well. Both women had been seen going to the departure gate, so I assumed they were on board. I'm not on that ship, so I couldn't check, but this is why we use the motorbike as a check-up. Where did it go wrong?"

"We thought the ladies had gone on board after John had watched them go into the terminus, that's what we usually do."

"Yes, I know that," said Gerald, getting quite short-tempered.

"It gets worse. One of our visitors was surprised when a woman sat up in bed and spoke to him. He hit her, and after checking her, I found she was dead."

"What a bloody mess. Theft is one thing but ending up with someone getting murdered is beyond belief."

"I'm feeling the same way. I didn't get a wink of sleep last night."

"And I won't tonight. Are you sure she's dead?"

"Well, I checked her for a pulse, but there was nothing. There was just lots of blood all around her head."

"What did he hit her with?"

"A bronze sculpture. He was trying to get the matching one on the other side of the bed when she woke up. Frightened the wits out of the lad. He panicked and just hit out with the statue he was holding."

"Well, they will be worth something to offset this debacle. Did you get the watch collection?"

What the hell? The heartless bugger. The old girl's dead, but all he's thinking of is the loot. "No, I didn't see much worthwhile at all. We left as soon as I'd checked the old woman." There was a long silence. "What are we going to do about this? How can we get this sorted out?"

Gerald huffed. "We? No, no. Not we—*you*. This is down to you. Robert, but I'm sure if the price is right, you'll get it sorted out. Just sell the stuff and transfer my share into my bank account, then close everything down. Our partnership is dissolved. Oh, and don't let my share of the profits go missing. I really do have some connections in the dark world and could arrange them to call."

"If I go down, you go with me. If you turn your back on me now and it goes wrong, I'll tell them you were my partner."

"Who's going to believe you? I'm on a ship in the middle of the Caribbean. How could I have gone into the house and aided the murderer? Sorry, Robert, but the problem is all yours. Bye." And he hung up.

"So much for honour amongst thieves," muttered Robert.

CHAPTER TWENTY-ONE

June / July

Just as morning had arrived for Robert, Sheila slowly opened her eyes and let her vision return. Her head was aching, and she was feeling weak. She lay still, letting her senses come fully to her, but her head was hurting so very much. She touched her head, and the pain caused her to jerk in her bed. "Damn COVID."

She lay still, then noticed her fingers were damp. She lifted her hand and looked at the red stain on her fingers and hand. Blood!

How? Could COVID do that?

After a while, she remembered the intruder and how he'd hit her.

I must get help, but can I move? Will it cause more damage? All sorts of questions went through her mind.

Gritting her teeth, she moved slowly sideways, feeling sick, and picked up her phone from the top of the cabinet. She was feeling faint, and the pain in her head was now at an almost unbearable level. She tried to stay focused, but everything began to spin. Still she managed to speed dial Gill.

"Hello, you must be feeling much better," Gill said.

For a short while, Sheila couldn't reply. She pulled on all her reserves and whispered, "Come quickly. Call an ambulance."

"What's happened?"

Again, that swirling effect delayed her response, but her foggy vision slowly returned. In a much-pained voice, she said, "Can't talk. Hurry. Help."

Then everything turned black, and Sheila descended into unconsciousness and dropped the phone.

Gill quickly pulled on her coat and shoes and rushed to Sheila's house. She let herself in and called out, "Where are you?" as she checked downstairs. She went upstairs to

Sheila's bedroom, stopped at the door and put her hand to her mouth when she saw Sheila in a bloody heap on the bed.

Barely able to control her fear, she rang 999 for an ambulance. She waited for what seemed an hour but was just a few moments before a voice asked, "What service do you require?"

Gill blurted out, "I think my friend is dead. I need an ambulance."

"Please stay calm, caller, and tell me what's happened."

Gill took a deep breath. "I think my friend has been killed by someone. I've just found her in a pool of blood in her bed."

"Thank you, caller. Can I take your name? And please stay on the line. I'll come back to you once I sort out the ambulance and notify the police."

Gill gave the control centre lady her name. "I had a phone call from Sheila asking me to come to her house. She sounded desperate. I thought it was to do with her COVID, but this is nothing to do with it."

"Are you with her at the moment?"

"I am, yes. I'm stood by the bedroom door."

"Can you describe what you can see, please? Where is the blood coming from? Her head, or her chest? Can you tell?"

Gill moved into the bedroom slowly. "I can see there's a lot of blood all over the pillow, so I think it must be a head wound. But I can't see it, and she's got some blood on her hand too."

"Okay. Please don't try to move her," the call centre lady said.

"Oh, I won't do that, but I'm now stood by the bed, holding her hand."

"I know it's hard, but I'd like you to go downstairs and watch for the ambulance. As soon as they come, then tell me, but until then, stay on the line, please."

Gill leaned close to Sheila's face and said, "If you can hear me Sheila, then please, oh, please, hang in there." She wasn't sure if Sheila was alive or dead, but she went downstairs, unhappy to leave her friend there. "Could you notify Detective Inspector Wainwright of Southampton central police station, please? We were both cooperating with him on a matter of mutual concern, and I think this is going to tie in with those investigations."

"Yes, I can do that. Stay on the phone while I try to get through to him." After a few moments, she came back. "He's on his way. They picked up on the earlier call for the police to attend."

The first to arrive was an ambulance, and Gill told the control centre lady, whom she thanked and then closed the line. Gill met the two paramedics and informed them that Sheila had been resting as she had COVID.

The team were wearing masks, and the one carrying a folded stretcher, asked, "Can you show us where your friend is, please,? And it might be wise for you put a mask on." Once outside of the bedroom, the same one said, "Thank you. If you could wait here by the door, that would be of help."

She watched as they checked for a pulse.

"Your friend is alive, but she is very weak."

Still standing at the door, Gill watched as they checked Sheila's head. They placed a stretcher at her side and lifted her head and the pillow while one of them supported her body. Then they asked if Gill could push the top part of the stretcher under her friend, so they could lift her onto it. Gill gladly did this small thing, as they lifted Sheila and made sure she didn't move. They then placed what looked like sandbags around Sheila.

"We need to get her into hospital as soon as we can," one said as they put straps around her friend to stop her moving. "I have to tell you that she's very weak and might not make it, but we're going to do our best to save her. Can you open the front door for us? We'll get her into the ambulance and get on our way."

They manoeuvred the stretcher downstairs and outside, then they slid the stretcher into the open doors at the back. One climbed into the back with Sheila and the other got into the driver's seat, and they took her away.

As she watched the ambulance disappear, Gill wondered if that would be the last time she was going to see her friend alive. *If you die, Sheila, I'll spend the rest of my life searching for the people who did this to you. I will not rest until vengeance is done.*

D.I. Wainwright arrived ten minutes later with a female constable whom he introduced as P. C. Gilmore. "Can you give me an idea what happened and what you think has occurred, please?"

Gill went back over with the way she'd ended up in Sheila's house after receiving a call from her. "I think she must have passed out, because the line was still open, and the phone was on the floor."

"I'd like to see the room, please," he asked and Gill escorted him upstairs to the room.

"Sheila was laying on the far side of the bed in a pool of blood."

"Do you know where your friend keeps the teabags?" D. I. Wainwright asked. "Because I could do with a cup, and I'm sure you and Alice could too."

As Gill went back downstairs, he pulled on thin rubber gloves and put on rubber shoe guards over his shoes. *This isn't a murder scene yet, but it could be.* He checked the room but couldn't see any sign of a knife or a blunt instrument that could have been used to strike Sheila.

He looked in all the other upstairs rooms, then went downstairs. "I've called the crime squad, and they'll be here soon, but so will the papers. For the moment, this isn't a violent crime scene. I'm going to say that we believe she fell down the stairs."

"But why? She clearly didn't do that."

"Someone falling down the stairs isn't very newsworthy and won't get a front-page mention. By diverting the true picture, it'll give us time to see how your tough friend Sheila gets through this. If it all goes wrong and we lose her, then I can rectify the statement and say we now think it was a robbery gone wrong. Much better to give us and your friend a little time."

"Yes, I can see that now," said Gill. "I've never been good at this subterfuge thing, but if the paper reporter asks me, can I just say that I'm far too upset to answer any pointless questions? Would that do?"

"That would do nicely. Now, I need to ring a few people to make sure that the news doesn't leak out. The hospital, for one. I have a few contacts there who can help dampen the news ferrets' lust for a story."

He rang a couple of people and gave out instructions. When his crime squad team arrived, he had a word with them then left them to it.

Gill sat in Sheila's favourite chair for no other reason than to feel close to her. They drank their cup of tea, and as they finished, a man came downstairs. "No sign of a knife or any blunt instrument, gov. They must have taken it with them."

"What about the two bronze statues on each side of the bed," asked Gill. "Did you check them?"

"No, ma'am. There's nothing on either cabinet."

"That will be it then," Gill said. "I didn't notice they weren't there; I was more concerned with Sheila. She had them for her wedding anniversary, one was a half man, half horse and the other was a half woman, half horse. I remember when they showed them to me. They were a pair from a limited edition of only one hundred. They will have a substantial value. They cost just short of a thousand pounds back then, but what they'll be worth now, I shudder to think. Sheila loved them. She told me she would touch the one on her husband's side of the bed and say goodnight to him."

"But she told me she had nothing of any value in her house when I asked."

"I think Sheila thinks of them as having sentimental value."

"I've checked the cameras, sir, but there's nothing on them."

D.I. Wainwright nodded. "This is Colin Harwood," he said to Gill. "He's one of my team members."

Before Gill could say anything, Colin said, "We've got to catch these bastards, gov. This is so wrong."

"Yes, Colin we should. Thank you for the update. Please go and help the rest of the team. I 'm going to make a few more calls."

Colin made his way back upstairs, and Gill waited as

Wainwright busied himself on the phone. She was almost to the point of tears.

PC Gilmore sat on the arm of the chair and put her arm around her. "If she's as tough as the inspector thinks she is, then she'll have a good chance."

She was distantly aware of PC Gilmore continuing to talk, but all Gill could think of was how Sheila was doing. Everything faded into a watery echo, like she was underwater.

And suddenly she wasn't. Inspector Wainwright asked. "Do you know what these statues were made of? Wood, metal, brass, anything like that?"

"Yes, I do know. They were solid bronze sculptures. I pointed that out to your man Colin when he came downstairs."

"So you did. Sorry, I didn't internalise that information. My mind is going from one point to another." He repeated the information down the phone, then thanked the person he was talking to and hung up.

They sat for almost an hour before the team that had been working upstairs came down. They had things bagged up, and they gave Gill a list of things they had removed from the room for her to give to Sheila if she survived or her next of kin if she didn't.

Once they'd gone, D.I. Wainwright said to Gill, "Will you lock the house up, and I'll give you a lift to your house. It's going to be hard over the next few days, but remember, say nothing, and we may get the envelope of time that we need to catch these evil people. Who could hit a defenceless woman with something, then steal the item and leave her to die. Would you like P. C. Gilmore to stay with you for a while?"

"No," Gill said, still on kind of autopilot. The last thing she wanted was to have to entertain a stranger in her own home.

D.I. Wainwright dropped her at her house, but before she got out of the car, he said, "I wonder why they went to her house first. You set the trap for them to visit your house, not Sheila's. I wonder if they got the wrong person?"

As the car drew away, Gill watched it turn at the top of the road. The two questions remained in her mind, *Why did they go to Sheila's house first and did they go to the wrong person?*

Then it hit her: if that was the case, Sheila should have been stood here, and it would be Gill fighting for her life.

***

It had been three days now since the visit to the house that had gone so horribly wrong, and Robert's nerves were all over the place. Surely she should have been found by now.

He'd arranged the removal of all the stolen items to go into a new lockup that had been bought to hide everything in case any questions arrived at his door. It had been purchased in another name, and it had taken almost a full day for him, Badger, and John to transfer everything.

Robert had cancelled the black auction, informing everyone that security was paramount, and that they'd discovered their site had been compromised. Gerald had made no further contact, and Robert assumed he was still on the cruise ship out in the Caribbean.

Robert had arranged to receive a daily electronic copy of the Southern Daily Echo, and with the help of John, he was able to read it on his TV screen. All he had to do was scroll down to get each page, one after the other. Nothing had been on the front page of the first three days' papers, nor anything inside. Most of the general information had been small local incidents: a local shop had been robbed; a woman had fallen down the stairs in her home and was likely to stay in the hospital for at least three days; a dog had been put down when it had bitten the postman; and two youths had been caught selling drugs. Nothing about a murder.

Stupidly, he found he hated the thought of the woman lying there rotting, with no one knowing she was lying in her bed, dead.

He went on with his legitimate businesses and the enquiries continued to increase, almost to the point that another removal van might be required. But he couldn't settle. Things kept coming back to him about that night. He didn't get nightmares, as such, but he never felt refreshed in the morning when he woke.

Each time he returned to his home above the garage,

he sat and looked around him. The cosy home, with all its imperfections, now looked drab and unkempt. Yes, it was the same place, but that last robbery had changed his whole outlook. So often in the last three days, he had asked himself the same question: why did I accept the partnership with Gerald Masters? And why didn't he stop everything when he found out that he was known as Gerald Portman?

When they moved everything from the storeroom, he washed the statue used by Billy to club the woman. He'd felt sick as he watched the blood drain down the sink.

The theft was one thing, but murder!

A tap on the door came and Badger entered. "You don't look good, guv. Why don't you take a sleeping pill or something? You've got to get some sleep."

"I know, Badger, but I keep thinking about that poor woman lying there with no one knows that she's dead. It's doing my head in."

"Yep, we're all upset about it, but what can we do to put it right? The answer is nothing. So, get a sleeping pill in you, guv, and get some rest."

"You seem remarkably calm about all this, Badger."

"Not at all, gov. To tell the truth, I'm a bag of nerves. I keep wondering if they ever found out it was us, what would happen to John? My son in prison as an accessory to murder. Me, well I would do my time, but my son? It cuts me to pieces thinking about it."

Robert put his arm around his friend. "You're right, Badger. We can't put the clock back, so we must carry the burden with us and hope that by acting normally, the cops don't get any information about it from any of us. How's Billy holding up?"

"He's not said much at all since that night. John has been going around to his house to see him every now and then."

"Let's hope he continues like that then. Now then, the jobs for today—that's what you came for, isn't it? Keep our heads down, run the legit business as usual, and try not to worry about the other one that went so wrong."

But I still hate to think of that poor woman laying rotting in her bed.

CHAPTER TWENTY-TWO

July

D.I. Wainwright sat at his desk and scratched his receding hairline as he read the missive in front of him.

Twenty days had passed since the almost-fatal robbery had occurred, and there'd been no more burglaries that matched the format of the perpetrators he was interested in. Interestingly, his opposite number hadn't reported any either. Had the gang been spooked by the near-miss and were taking a break to wait for things to calm down?

The message in front of him, related to the events, had caused D.I. Wainwright to raise his eyebrow.

They'd put a search out for the next port of call for the Saga cruise ship, but when they asked for confirmation that one of their dance hosts, Gerald Portman, was still on the ship, the purser messaged back that he hadn't returned to the ship in Antigua. He had contacted the ship and reported to them that he was unwell and was going into hospital for a check-up. He'd said he was sorry about this but hoped to catch up with the cruise ship in the near future. In response to the request for information for the hospital Gerald Portman was in, the Antiguan police said they had no record of a Gerald Portman in any hospital on Antigua, and they had no idea if he was still on the island.

So what the hell was going on? They needed to talk to him. This case was getting more and more puzzling as it went on. His chief inspector wanted to issue a true statement about Sheila's incident, and with Gerald Portman disappearing, no matter how much D. I. Wainwright fought against it, it looked as if the truth was going to be made public. He needed a bloody miracle, and he'd always been a little short on the arrival of those.

***

Gill had been in touch with the hospital most days but was shocked by how gaunt and pale Sheila was when she was finally allowed to visit her friend with Robin, Sheila's son, who had flown over from Australia to be by her side. Tubes and pipes were coming out from her mouth, nose, and from beneath the bed covers. Sheila wasn't moving at all, and the machine was drawing air and pumping it into her, causing her chest to rise and fall.

The doctor explained that she was in an induced coma, and they had pinned her skull as a piece had pressed against her brain. He said that they were now reducing the drugs that kept her in a comatose state, and they hoped for a slow but successful recovery.

"Tell me, doctor, what are Mum's chances?"

The reply was rather long but with a studied knowledge.

"Anyone in a comatose state is at risk of dying. In some cases, there may be a complete recovery with no loss of brain functioning, while in other cases, lifelong brain damage is the result. The chances of someone recovering from a coma largely depend on the severity and the cause of their brain injury. In your mother's case, it was a violent blow to the side of her head, and a small piece of her skull pressing against the brain had caused swelling. Her age can also be a problem factor. The longer she remains in a coma, induced or not, adds to the problem of recovery. It's impossible to accurately predict whether she will eventually recover, or whether she'll have any long-term problems. Your mother is reasonably fit for her age, and we're hopeful that she will recover, but to what state, we'll only be able to determine once she opens her eyes. Meanwhile, keep talking to her, and report to me or any nurse nearby if her eyelids start to flutter."

Robin and Gill had drunk a bottle of wine together after they had returned back to her house where he was staying. Unashamedly, both had shed tears over this news.

The following day, Gill sat beside Sheila's bed and held her hand. "You have me to talk to you today. Robin has a lot of paperwork to do, something to do with the legal responsibility, so he's with your bank manager sorting out how to still go on paying your bills." She rubbed the back of Sheila's hand, looking at the face of her friend as she lay helpless.

"All of the dance club members send their best wishes to you, even Arthur Walters—who you've landed me with—sent you a card. If this is a cunning plan to force me to dance with him, then I have to tell you, it worked. I did a quickstep with him last week to 'Shall we dance' from the film *The King and I*, and it was a lovely *walk* around the floor."

She looked at Sheila and swallowed down the sudden urge to cry. That wouldn't help Sheila at all. So, she went on talking, telling her about little things that had happened, how the weather was changing—one week hot, the next rain. It was all terribly mundane, but it was important to Gill to do her bit to help Sheila's recovery.

She'd been there for almost two hours when a nurse asked her if she could go into the waiting room because they would be working with the doctor in a few moments, and they needed access to all sides of the bed.

Reluctantly, Gill let go of her friend's hand and made her way out of Sheila's room. She took advantage of the restroom before sitting, and seeing a pile of magazines, she decided to try to concentrate on one of those.

She had no idea how long she would have to wait, but until Sheila was sitting beside her, even if it felt like eternity, she would wait.

***

D.I. Wainwright listened to the report from his counterpart D.I. Harris, who covered the southern area to Dover and with whom he had liaised with since the first contact with his granny sleuths. "That's great, D.I. Harris, thank you. Can you email it to me so I can pass it along the chain?"

He ended the call and said to Sandra, "Once the copy comes through from the East Coast office, can you make two copies, one for the files and the other for me? Then you and I are going to need to get our heads together to figure this thing out, because our leads are blown to bits and are now resting on a woman in a coma."

"No problem." Sandra left her desk to go to the main printer. She returned, having skimmed over the message quickly, and waited for her boss to start the discussion about it.

"Well, that's a bombshell, isn't it?"

"Yes, it is. If Gerald Portman is dead, who is the man who's taken his identity?" said Sandra.

"Yes, in a nutshell, that's the question."

"What a good bit of policing the East Coast did on this. If they hadn't done any research into the name of Gerald Portman, we would never have known that he had been killed during the invasion of Iraq along with US troops in 2003."

The police had contacted Sir Arthur Portman, the well-known import/exporter, and he'd told them his son had died. Quite rightly, he was appalled to hear that someone was impersonating his son.

The concluding line in the report was a shocker: "With the gang now gone to ground in both your area and mine, and as we're not getting any reports of burglaries associated with cruise victims, all of our leads have gone with the disappearance of the person purporting to be Gerald Portman."

Sandra watched her boss tap his teeth with a pencil, as he did so often when thinking through various points to an investigation that had a problem to it.

D.I. Wainwright leaned forward. "I wonder if our mysterious man is on our database. Perhaps he left something in his cabin that we could get some fingerprints or DNA from to track him down."

"Shall I message the ship and ask them to check his cabin?"

"Yes, Sandra, and tell them that everything should be handled with gloves and not their bare hands. They should try to not smudge things as they bag them, and they need to bag *everything,* no matter how inconsequential or small they might think it is." He sat back and began tapping his teeth again. *Maybe, just maybe, we'll get lucky.*

CHAPTER TWENTY-THREE

July/ August

D.I. Wainwright looked at the message he had received from the cruise ship's hotel director who was responsible for the overall operation of the hotel department on the ship.

He reported that he'd had no more contact from Gerald Portman, and as he was sharing a cabin, they had asked the other dance host to pack all his belongings up, and they would put him in another cabin.

They had instructed him not to touch anything that might belong to Gerald Portman and had watched the man pack his things and then had locked the door behind him as he went to his new cabin.

The ship was almost in Cuba and was due to arrive the next evening. and could they expect someone to come aboard to supervise the collection of items that may have been touched by Gerald Portman?

It message ended with "It is very distressing to hear that he's a suspect linked to a murder, and we'll do everything to help the police, but would appreciate a low profile, as shocking publicity can cause all sorts of negative results, like a drop in bookings.

He emphasised that they would cooperate as much as they could to help the police.

The ship would end its cruise at Fort Lauderdale, and the passengers would be taken to the airport and then fly home to many countries.

D.I. Wainwright had the authority to send out two forensic crime experts from the C.I.D. who would check everything and bag up any items that they thought would bring a lead.

Now it was just a waiting game.

***

Gill sat beside the bed, once again holding Sheila's hand.

The drugs they had been giving Sheila were now almost withdrawn, and they were expecting to see some sign that she was going to wake up.

Once again, the warning that she might not do that and that she could die when they turned off the machines didn't do much for Robin and Gill's morale.

Four more weeks had passed, and there'd been no sign of life from her.

Robin, who sat on the other side of the bed, let go of his mother's hand and stood up. "I'm going to get a cup each of that appalling coffee and a couple of biscuits for us."

Gill looked up at him, nodded and then looked at Sheila. "Robin, stop. Talk about the coffee again; I'm sure Sheila's lips moved."

He sat quickly and took hold of Sheila's hand. "Mum, if you can hear me, would you like to join us in drinking one of the foulest cups of coffee I've ever tasted?"

Both were staring at Sheila when her lips quivered slightly and the tip of her tongue tip poked through the slight gap.

"Oh, Mum, you're coming back to us." Tears ran down his cheeks as he smiled at Gill, who was just as bad as him.

Gill pressed the button that would bring the doctors and nurses to the room, and her heart lurched as she realised how long she'd waited, desperate to press that button.

A nurse came in and checked Sheila, then pressed a button on the side panel and said that the doctor would be there very soon.

In a very short time, a doctor and two juniors arrived, and Robin and Gill were asked to leave so that they could do some tests on Sheila's responses.

Once again, they sat in the waiting room, watching a minute hand on the clock seemingly take an hour for just one minute to pass.

It was, however, a long wait, and at last, a nurse arrived. "All done now. If you'd like to return to Mrs Chancel's bedside, I think you'll be pleased that you waited."

They found that Sheila still had a mask on, and tubes and pipes still came from her. Her head was slightly raised on two pillows, and a long single pillow seemed to be supporting her shoulders.

But her chest was rising and falling on its own. The breathing apparatus had been removed, and Sheila was breathing for herself!

***

"Sorry, Badger, I drifted away again as you were talking."

"You're doing that a lot lately, boss. Are you still dwelling on that job and the old woman?"

"Yes, Badger, I am. It was about nine weeks ago. She must be stinking the house out by now. Why haven't they found her yet?"

"Maybe she hasn't got anyone to find her, guv. Not every old person has their kith and kin nearby."

"But she went with a friend on holiday. Why hasn't she raised the alarm? No, Badger, something isn't quite right with this, and I'm beginning to think there's a cover-up going on. I thought she was dead, but I'm no doctor. What if she isn't?"

"But you felt for a pulse and said you couldn't find any."

"As I said, Badger, I'm no doctor, but my logic says someone should have found her by now."

Badger looked at the man sitting behind his desk; he certainly didn't look as worried as he had been. Thinking about it, what he was saying had credence to it. "Billy would certainly feel a lot better if the old woman is alive."

"I'll bet he would," Robert said. "What was her name? Can you remember?"

"One was Gill something, the other was something like Shirley Channel. I can find out for you. We still have the addresses and names in our book in the new storage unit."

"Yes, we do, don't we?" Robert suddenly felt more energised and better than he had for over two months. If the old woman was still alive, he'd feel a damn sight better too. "Right, leave that to me. You get on with the loading of the Luxton's furniture this afternoon, and I'll slip up to the new unit and check on their names."

"Right, guv. Best of luck. See you in the morning." Badger turned and left Robert in his office living area. He descended the stairs to the garage where the two other lads were waiting for him.

They opened the garage doors, and as the removal van cleared the doors, Badger touched the button to close them and just like Elvis, he left the building.

***

Sheila opened her eyes slowly, her vision very blurry. She lay still, aware that lights were on around her… Had she gone to sleep with the bedroom light on? As her focus cleared, she looked around without moving her head. Where was she? Not in her bedroom. A shopping mall? Had she fallen and bumped her head?

Voices were coming through the confusion, and again she tried to concentrate on what was being said.

She tried to move but couldn't. Was she tied down? Panic bubbled up. Again, she tried but couldn't move, then a blurred face came close to hers and a soft voice said, "It's all right, Mrs Chancel. You're in hospital, and you're in safe hands. Now try to relax and once you feel a little better, we will try to lift you slightly to let you look around."

Hospital? Why? So many questions ploughed through her foggy mind.

Her vision was starting to clear, and more and more, things around her began to come into focus.

The man who had spoken to her, stood near the bed, well within her sight without her turning her head.

"Can you see my face clearly now, Mrs Chancel? You won't be able to speak for a while. Your brain is just waking up and trying to respond to your actions and the responses you want it to do. You can move your fingers, so if you can see my face clearly, try blinking your eyes once or twice for no."

Sheila stared at the man, and then the question came back into her mind, and she blinked once.

"Excellent. Don't worry about the time delay. You're doing very well. Do you have a headache?"

After a moment, Sheila again blinked once.

"Very good. I will arrange for a nurse to give you an injection that will slowly take the pain away, and you will probably go to sleep. I'll see you again a little later."

A nurse stepped up close to Sheila and did something to her arm, and as she watched the nurse walk away, her eyes slowly closed, and soon she returned to a blessed sleep.

***

When Badger came into the garage the following day, Robert was waiting for him.

"You have a short run today using the lorry. It's a delivery of cases to a company that has been promised same-day delivery, but the driver of Casters and Sons' vehicle has been involved in an accident. Take John with you. Transfer the cargo into the lorry and deliver the cases to their client ASAP. Fortunately, none of the bottles of wine broke, but be careful how you handle it. And *no* samples. Tonight, we're going to visit Partner's house to see what's in there or if he's at home."

"It'll surprise him if he is. Us turning up will be the last thing he's expecting."

"It will surprise me if he's there too. I'm expecting the house to be quite bare, but we'll see."

***

Once again, Sheila eased into the world, but her sight returned much quicker than it had a few moments ago. She looked around and saw a nurse. "Nurse," she said in a rather drunken voice.

The nurse turned and came over to Sheila. "Hello, sleepy head. You're looking better this morning."

Morning? When did I go to sleep? The doctor told a nurse to give me some painkiller medicine. Did they also put sleeping drugs into me? She licked her lips, then forced a reply, "How…long…have…I…been…here?" Each word was an effort, and her headache was returning.

"The doctor will answer all your questions soon, but for

now, just relax and rest. Is your headache starting again?"

"Yes."

She turned, walked back to her trolley, and returned with a tray. She placed it on the bed, did something to whatever was on it, and then Sheila felt her arm being lifted. Slowly, her eyes closed, and she sank into sleep once again. The nurse adjusted the drips at the side of the bed, looked at her watch, and wrote notes on a chart at the end of the bed.

She smiled at Sheila and then returned to her trolley to deal with her next patient.

CHAPTER TWENTY-FOUR

August

D.I. Wainwright looked at the list of just two items that had been found in the cabin that the other dance host, Martyn Peters, said had nothing to do with him. The man they knew as Gerald Portman had been very thorough. The team weren't sure if the items would provide any help, but both had definitely been handled by the man they wanted to find.

Mr Peters had provided them with a set of his fingerprints, and they had assured him that they would be destroyed once they had eliminated his prints on the folder with note paper, envelopes, and other odd bits inside it. Both men had handled it, and Mr. Peters was sure it was Gerald who had used it last. He'd said he was checking his flight times for his return after the cruise. They reported that the indentation on the sheet of the notepad may give a phone number; they were having that checked now and would report back.

The other thing was a pack of cards, which they'd played poker with on a few evenings when there was no dancing. Both sets of fingerprints could be on those.

It could be nothing, but it could also be everything.

Sandra returned to the office and smiled. "Our granny sleuth Sheila is a fighter. She's getting stronger and is making progress, but it's slow. They said she's still having headaches, and they had to sedate her. She's having a brain scan at the moment, but the swelling is subsiding and they are quietly confident that she'll recover, but to what extent, they couldn't say."

"So we aren't going to get a description just yet." He sat forward in his chair, which made more noise than usual.

"No. At this rate, it could be months. Are you sure you don't want me to get another chair from downstairs? That one doesn't sound very healthy at all."

Inspector Wainwright leaned back into it, swivelled, and

rested his left leg on the desk. "It's fine, Sandra. It's just having a bad day, like me."

Sandra left her boss and closed the door to the office, knowing that he would be going over the case again, looking for something—anything—that could crack it.

***

At two o'clock in the morning, Badger and Robert entered Gerald's house through the rear door. It had no security lock on it, was poorly maintained, and had taken only a few minutes to open.

They walked through the kitchen, which was spartan, to say the least. There wasn't even a kettle in sight. The lounge was even worse: no chair, no TV, nothing. It was just an empty shell. The bedrooms were the same, with no bed or furniture in any of them.

"He doesn't live here, Badger. This is just a front. I have no idea now where the hell he could be."

They left the house and returned to base.

"What's going on, guv?" asked Badger as his boss poured out a whisky for them both.

"I don't know, Badger. I wish I did, but if the police aren't looking for him, then it's us that are going to be their next target. Fortunately, they don't seem to be aware of our existence."

Little did he know that was about to change!

***

D.I. Wainwright listened to his superior and then put his idea to him once again, making sure that he stressed the benefits of the action. "If we make the announcement this way, two things could occur. One, we get a lead on the person we know as Gerald Portman, and second, the gang will panic at the wording 'attempted murder.' I can alert my opposite number, and we can then both watch out for any odd response from the public or one of the villains. I've also requested a list of people leaving Antigua and St. Martin, the nearest island to

Antigua, who made a last-minute booking. That should come through in a few days."

"Very well. Make the announcement in the paper, and let's hope you're right. What happened with the cards and the notepad from the ship?"

"The cards didn't provide anything like a fingerprint, but the notepad gave us a number, which turned out to be a travel agent's in Bermuda. We contacted them, but they couldn't give us any information. They said they hadn't sold any plane tickets to a solo passenger. All their recent sales had been for tour groups."

"Another lost lead then."

The inspector returned to his room and asked Sandra to ring Chris Foreman, the newshound for the local paper. "Tell him we have a scoop for him. That should set him running to us."

Within an hour, Chris Foreman was listening to what D. I. Wainwright was saying and couldn't believe his ears. *The Echo* was getting this police request first before it went to all the other papers. He took the statement from him and thanked him.

"You've helped us before, Chris, so I thought you'd like to put your name to it and then let the other newspapers pick it up," said D.I. Wainwright. "Then you'll get the credit for the scoop."

He looked at the statement, then stood and shook hands with the inspector. Sandra escorted him to the exit. She returned to the office with a cup of tea for her boss.

"Let's hope we get some results on this," he said, "because we still have nothing else."

***

Another day passed, and when Sheila opened her eyes, she seemed to focus almost at once. She ran her tongue around her mouth, which felt like the inside of a birdcage, and looked around for a nurse. No one was in sight, but after a few moments, a nurse came to her bed.

"Well, you've had a good sleep. How do you feel today?"

Today. Do they drug me and put me out for a whole day? "I feel much better," she said.

The nurse smiled. "Yes, and your coordination is coming back. Your speech is so much better today."

"Can you tell me why I'm here, please? I have no idea. Did I faint and bump my head or something while I was shopping?"

"You had a head injury, and it took quite a long time to sort it out. If you could hold onto your questions, I'll get the doctor."

The nurse left Sheila lying on the bed with lots of questions and no one to ask.

***

The first of August didn't just sweep in with rain and wind, it brought in a shock for Robert. He had made his first cup of tea for the morning while downloading *The Echo*, as he'd got in the habit of doing.

The headline on the front page caused him to spill his tea.

Attempted Murder Hunt.

Police hunt for a man known as Gerald Portman in conjunction with a suspected attempted murder investigation.

It went on to describe how the man had adopted the son's name of Sir Arthur Portman, a well-known import/exporter. Sir Arthur's son was killed during the invasion of Iraq while fighting alongside the US troops in 2003.

The man's last occupation was as a dance host aboard various holiday cruise ships.

Police are requesting to make contact with anyone who has had dealings with this man and who may have socialised with him.

If you know him or know of his whereabouts, please contact D.I Wainwright.

Robert read it three times before it finally dawned on him that the old dear wasn't dead, after all.

Somehow, he was very pleased about this, but now things had changed. Now they were no longer thieves in the night, now they the fox, and the hounds were on the hunt.

The following day, Robert's premonition was confirmed. All of the local papers had picked up the police request, and Detective Inspector Harris of the southeast division also had confirmed that they had an interest in the whereabouts of the same man. His number had also been added to the original number posted.

Four people who read this at the same time as Robert, who managed to drink his morning tea without spilling any this time, had different reactions to it.

Charlie Evans read this and wondered if he should contact Robert to ask if he should volunteer the knowledge that he'd gathered. After giving it some though, he did nothing about it. If Robert wanted to help the police, he had the means, but it wasn't up to him.

Fredrick Winterbottom, a politician, gave thought to this article not as to how he could help with their enquiries, but how it would seem if it came out that he knew Gerald Portman as a friend and as a dealer. If it turned out that the paintings or anything he'd brought to him for consideration turned out to be stolen, his world would soon come crashing down too. He decided to not rush into anything but decided to get a friend in the CID to keep him unofficially informed.

The man known as Gerald Portman aka Gerald Masters also read the newspaper and cursed the day he had ever tied in with Robert Price. He reread the piece and cursed again. There was no mention of any other people they wanted; just him in conjunction with an attempted murder. But he'd been on a cruise ship. Why had that fact not stopped the plods from laying the near death of the old lady at his door. At least their worst fears had not been substantiated; they hadn't killed her as that idiot Priceright had thought.

What should he do?

He opened a drawer in a cabinet by his side and pulled out a mobile phone. He switched it on, put in the number he wanted and waited for the recipient to reply.

"Hello," said Robert.

"Have you read today's papers?"

Robert recognised Gerald's voice at once. "No nice to speak to you again, or are you well? Bit too much to expect, I suppose, from someone who told me I was on my own when we last spoke. Well today, you're on your own. Goodbye."

"Wait," Gerald shouted. "If I get caught, you do too."

Robert paused, his finger hovering over the red disconnect button. He lifted the phone to his ear. "You really are a shit, aren't you?"

"If I am, then you're going to join me in it."

"Okay, I'm listening. What are you proposing?"

"First, any idea how they got onto me? I hope you haven't done something stupid like putting the cops on my tail."

"No. Unlike you, I wouldn't do that. How about the two people you gave us the addresses of last, the one who we found in her bed? That was a lot of disinformation, wasn't it?"

"No, it wasn't. That information was correct, but because of COVID restrictions, they didn't board. I contacted Mark, a dance host on the Fred Olsen ship, and he explained that several people had been refused boarding, and both of our clients were among those. I only found out after you informed me that you'd killed the woman. Incidentally, who was it you thought you'd killed? Was it the tall one?"

"No, she was the shorter of the two. The tall one was our target for the watches."

"So, another mistake. You couldn't even get that right. I told you which one to visit, but no, that seems to have been too hard for your moron to grasp. So you went to the wrong house, didn't you?"

"It could've been the same result even if we'd gone to the right house. We would have found the other one in bed."

"We'll never know now, will we?" said Gerald.

"I didn't get the caller signal when you rang. Where are you now?"

"If you think I'm going to answer that, think on. I'm calling from a burner phone. The last thing I want is for you to help the police."

"I have already told you: I don't do that sort of thing."

"How about that photo you took of me? Could one of your crew plant that for the police to find and turn attention to me."

"I don't have a photo of you. I never did. That was a bluff to warn you that I'm no pushover."

"Really? Well, that should help." And he rang off.

***

The fourth person who'd read the article looked at the paper for a long, long time, and after giving it an awful lot of thought, she wrote the phone number down on a pad.

Helen Prescott sat back in her chair and reread the words that had shocked her.

Attempted Murder Hunt.

The police were hunting for a man *known as* Gerald Portman in conjunction with a suspected *attempted murder investigation.* She underlined the two parts that shocked her. *And then there was the part where he had adopted a dead man's name. No wonder he wouldn't marry me; he couldn't.*

Attempted murder. She'd let this person seduce her into bed, and no matter how good he was, she'd slept with a suspected murderer. Had he slept with another woman and tried to kill her? The article didn't state if the victim was a woman or a man. Helen just hadn't seen him as a killer.

She'd known him as an art and painting go-between, not a dance host. How demeaning that second job must have been, but he'd told the truth when he said he did a lot of travelling around the world. Helen had thought it was after paintings or some artwork, but no, dancing around the world was more truthful.

She reread the bit about the police wanting anyone who had socialised with him to come forward, and she made up her mind. *I guess deep and satisfying sex could be considered socialising.*

She picked up her phone.

CHAPTER TWENTY-FIVE

August

Sheila sat up in her bed, pillows all around her, and a high guard rail along the length of the bed on both sides. She smiled as Robin and Gill came into the room.

After the exchange of kisses and tender hugs, the obvious questions came.

"My goodness, Mum, you can't imagine how much joy it gives me to see how you look now."

Sheila assured them that she was definitely feeling much better, and then said, I had a brain scan early this morning that apparently confirmed that the swelling had gone down quite dramatically, which might explain why my headaches are almost non-existent.

"Have the doctors told you about the operation?" Gill asked. "And do you remember much about it?"

"Yes," said Sheila, "the doctor informed me that I'd been hit on the side of my head by someone who was in my bedroom. He was a thief who must have disturbed me while I slept, and he hit me as I woke. I have no recollection of this so far, but I keep getting flashbacks. We," she pointed to Gill, "were going to go on a cruise together, but for some reason, we didn't go. That came back to me as I waited to go into the machine for them to look at my brain. They took my bandages off this morning. I have no hair! And, stupidly, I don't remember what colour it was or if it was straight or curly."

Robin held his mother's hand. "You're on the mend, Mum, and that's the most important thing. The doctors told me that the flashbacks are your brain locating memories and placing them with other memories. Gradually, things will come together, and you'll be back to where you were before."

"Yes, Robin, I know." She smiled. "They said the same to me." She turned to Gill. "Are you still going to the club for the afternoon tea dance?"

"Yes, I have, and everyone sends their best wishes to you for a speedy recovery."

"I have some difficult news for you, Mum," said Robin. "I have to go back to Australia tomorrow. You're through the worst, but I have to return to my family and business in Oz. So we'll be back to the connection on our phones or computers."

Shelia squeezed his hand, and tears started to run down her cheeks. "I know, Robin. You have your own life now, and you must get back to it. Once I'm up and walking around, I'd like to come down under to visit you, Mavis, and the grandchildren. Don't worry, I'll be all right. As you said, I'm on the mend, and given a month or two, should be up and about. Let's see if I can come to you for Christmas. You've both been asking me to come, so if you ask this year, you already know the answer will be yes."

Robin kissed her. "Oh behalf of the Australian branch of the Chancel family, I am asking."

They hugged and kissed, before Robin turned to Gill. "You have the same invitation, Gill. We wouldn't want to split up a team like you two."

Gill beamed at him. "I'd love to."

Robin noticed his mother frowning. "What's up, Mum?"

"I've just had a vision; I saw the youth that hit me. My head—he hit my head as I sat up. It was the statue. He had the statue by the bed and he was looking at it, and then he said something. That's when I woke up."

"Oh, Mum, I hope you aren't getting pains with these recall visions. Shall I call the nurse?"

"No, I'm fine, Robin. It's so strange how a part of my memory has returned from nothing. There seems to be no logic at all. We were talking about Christmas, and suddenly, bang, I was sitting in bed with an intruder beside me. One thing's for sure, I'd recognise him in a crowd."

***

Helen picked up her phone and rang the police. It wasn't a call centre, as she'd expected, but an answering service. She listened to the questions and then gave the answers.: name, address, her phone number, and a brief statement of how and when she knew Gerald Portman.

The system then informed her that someone would contact her in the near future, and she hung up.

It was a bit of an anti-climax, really, but she could understand it. There would be all sorts of calls, and they would need to weed the good calls from the rest. She would just have to be patient and wait until they contacted her.

Nothing happened for two days, and Helen had all but forgotten the phone call to the police. She was running through a brochure with the lists and photographs of the items for the next auction when her mobile rang.

"Hello," she said.

"Good morning, madam. Am I speaking to Ms Helen Prescott?"

"You are, and to whom am I speaking?"

"Constable William Granger, ma'am. I'm returning your call in regard to the message you left about Gerald Portman."

"Ah, yes, constable, I did leave a message. And yes, I do know him. If you'd like to call around to my office at about two o'clock, I'll be able to spare some time to talk to you, but Christie's has an auction coming up very soon, and I'm busy going over that at the moment."

"Very well, I'm sure we'll be able to fit in with your wishes for that time. Are you sure your boss will allow you some time to talk to us?"

"Constable, I am one of Christie's chief advisors. I am a 'boss' as you call your superiors, and therefore, I'll be available to see you at the appointed time. Please check that you can have the time with your superior to come to see me. Good day." And in a huff, she hung up before the policeman could respond.

***

D.I. Wainwright was eating a biscuit as he gave thought to the way Gerald Portman could have left the country when Sandra returned to the office. He finished it and reached for another. "It's no good looking at me like that. I'll give them up and start the diet the doctor wants me to go on tomorrow, but until then, I must concentrate on emptying the box so that they won't go to waste."

"They wouldn't go to waste. You could pass them around to the rest of the team outside."

"But they'd get fat like me. No, I'm doing them a favour and finishing them to keep temptation out of their way." He started another one. "I wonder how our star witness is getting on. How do you fancy going to visit to see if she has any recall of the events that night? Ring first, just in case."

As Sandra turned to go, the phone rang so she took the call. "Yes, he's here at the moment. Could you put him through on line one, please?" She put her hand over the speaker. "Detective Inspector Harris from the southeast division wishes to speak to you."

He brushed crumbs from the desktop and pressed to answer the phone on speaker. "D.I. Wainwright."

"We had a call from a very good source today, and I've made an appointment to see a young lady who seems very disenchanted with our Gerald Portman. Her name is Helen Prescott, and she's an advisor at Christie's. She says that she, quote, 'knows him quite intimately,' close quote. I've taken over the interview from our local lad. She sounds like a formidable woman."

"So this could lead to a possible idea of where he is now."

"That's my feeling. Good idea of yours letting the papers hunt him. Now we have to hope for a result with this lady, who if I'm not mistaken, is the epitome of 'hell has no fury.' I'll keep you informed."

Wainwright replaced the phone and leaned back in his chair. "Well, maybe, just maybe, we will get a lead."

***

It was two days later when Gill visited Sheila to find the policewoman Sandra sat by the bed.

Sheila was sat up in the bed now, and although her colour had returned, and some of the tubes or pipes had gone, her head was still bandaged up.

Gill greeted Sandra then turned to Sheila and said, "Well, you're looking much better now, but you still have that bandage on your head."

"The doctors will be removing it tomorrow," Sheila said, "and they'll give me a chance to see the scar for myself and if any hair is growing back. I've also had a tube removed and can now go to the toilet pulling this stand." She pointed to the tall stand on wheels, which was connected to her arm. "But I'm getting stronger, and someday soon, they'll disconnect all of the pipework."

"It's all good news," said Sandra. "However, although most of your memory of that night and your earlier memories have returned, the description you gave me of your assailant isn't refined enough to point us in the right direction."

"Yes, I'm sorry about that. I wish I could do better, but it was so fleeting. I still say if I saw him again, I would know him."

"Never mind, you're getting better and stronger every day, and they'll soon get fed up with you and tell you to go home."

"Oh, I hope so. Thank you for coming in to see me and thank you for the grapes."

As Sandra left, Gill said, "Grapes? Goodness, you'll be expecting caviar soon."

"You mean you didn't bring me any? Oh, how the mighty have fallen."

They were laughing when the nurse came with another man, whom she introduced as Sheila's home coordinator. It would be his job to see if Sheila was fit enough to do small jobs once the home help service could be arranged.

"No need for that," said Gill. "Once Sheila can go home, she can move into my house for a while and if she needs care, I'll give it to her. She usually goes to sleep when we're having a conversation, so I can make sure she gets plenty of rest." She turned to Sheila. "You can practice getting the kettle on at my house and doing all the mundane chores we have to do, but once the doctors say you're well enough to be on your own, then I'll kick you out."

Sheila smiled. "After a single and very small glass of red wine, no doubt."

"You'll be taking pills, so you won't be having any, but I might let you sniff mine before I drink it," replied Gill.

They laughed, but the home coordinator looked baffled. "You did say you were friends, didn't you?"

Sheila turned to her and said, "Oh yes, we're always like this. A laugh or two helps the world go around, don't you think?"

The home coordinator looked from one to the other but still seemed at a loss.

"Never mind, dear," said Gill. "Take it that we're both pleased to be back together again, when at one time, I thought I might not see my dearest friend ever again."

And she wiped a tear from her eye, and Sheila did the same.

***

D. I. Harris met Helen Prescott at 2 o'clock in her office.

Once he had introduced himself, he said, "I felt that I should take over from my officer. I hope you weren't too upset by his remarks about superiors."

Helen smiled.

Having cleared that up, he said, "I have some questions for you."

But within minutes, Helen took over the interview. She told him about her relationship with Gerald Portman, as she knew him, and the fact that they had become lovers.

She then told him about the marriage v mistress proposition and how she'd thrown him out. "I haven't seen him since that day, and in light of the information I now have, I have no intention of becoming familiar with him again."

"Do you have any idea where he might be now?"

"I am afraid not. As to where he lived, I had no idea."

D. I. Harris left her with the knowledge that should Gerald Portman darken her doorstep, he would be informed.

***

D.I. Wainwright was a happy man. His request about any people leaving Antigua had drawn no results, but the message about the island of St. Martin came up trumps. They had someone who made a last-minute booking and had given him a prospective name. It wasn't Portman, but it was a name on the police database.

A last-minute booking had been made from St. Martin to fly from St Kitts, a nearby island. St. Kitts police had obtained a video copy that showed the man going through passport control. They also sent a passport number and name, and low and behold, the name was on the police database.

The chameleon has turned out to be none other than Gary Wickware, a well-known con man, who had spent some time behind bars after selling plots of land to unsuspecting purchasers who wanted to build their own homes on the plots. The problem had been that it wasn't his land, and no application had been put in for any building.

So he was now onto a long con but had set others up to do the work, and if they got caught, they would take the fall, and he would just disappear. But thanks to Wainwright's two determined ladies, the granny sleuths, Wickware had failed, and now they had a very strong lead.

He had put a call through to his opposite number, D. I. Harris, and he had welcomed the information. "I've sent the information through to your office."

"As you know, we had a phone call lead," D.I. Harris said. "I interviewed the lady myself. Helen Prescott knew the man known as Gerald Portman and remarked that he was not a man she would be welcoming in the future.'

They now needed a break, something to lead them to their man's door.

CHAPTER TWENTY-SIX

September

The Echo put a piece on the front page about a woman who had recovered from a brutal attack during an attempted robbery in her home. It reiterated that there was a reward for any information that would help the police.

Gill and Sheila read it, of course, but so did someone else, and although he was glad she wasn't dead, Robert now feared that she might be well enough to help the police find out Billy's name.

Robert had given thought to the possibilities of the area police forces cooperating but judging by past comments in newspapers about police areas cooperating, that wasn't very likely. The local police force in Southampton were likely to contain their investigations to their own area, thinking most likely, that the perpetrators of the theft were local to their region.

The article mentioned that police still wanted to interview Gerald Portman. The national newspapers picked it up a day later, but it only made print as a small fill-in piece on page five.

A few other people, however, did pick it up.

Helen Prescott sat in her office reading through the paper, having read the article about their last sale. A record amount had been exchanged for a painting, but the buyer had chosen not to allow his or her name during and after the transaction. Any publicity that was free was good publicity, as long as no confidences had been breached. When she came to the small piece about the robbery, she sat back and gave thought to the man she knew as Gerald Portman.

Damn. How could she fall for a piece of garbage like him?

As she finished her tea, a thought came to her, something that the fugitive had said to her in passing while they lay in bed together after a very satisfactory coupling. She finished her tea then went to a cupboard and pulled out her diaries for the last two years.

She came to the part that had prompted her to read her past scribbling.

After a superb dinner with Gerald, we walked back to the flat, and after we'd slowly undressed, drinking our champagne and giggling like children, we made slow and passionate love. That man really knows how to please a woman. One strange comment that Gerald made surprised me, however, and I have decided to record it. We were lying together in bed, and I asked him if we could go to his home sometime in the future for a change, and he said that his home was in Saudi Arabia, and that he uses hotels in every other country. Then he had said that if ever he wanted to settle in the UK, he would buy a narrowboat and move around in that, never staying in one place, always on the move. I asked him why he always wanted to be on the move, and he replied, "It's my restless spirit, and that would be a good name for it."

Helen wondered if he'd done just that…

***

The fugitive also picked up on the news article and smiled as he read it. Page five. They were getting tired of it as news. Soon he could resurface, get a new identity, and leave England to get on with his life once again.

***

An unsavoury character also read the article, but his attention fell on the word reward.

He had information about the gang who did this job, but how was he going to get his hands on the money before he gave them the information?

***

Robert looked out of his window at the blustery day and wondered where the year had gone. The promise of a hot summer hadn't materialised, as it often didn't, and most Brits had taken holidays abroad. Anything to get some sunshine.

As he got dressed, he thought about the article in the paper two days ago, and as he did each morning, thought of the offer of a reward for any information.

His mind went to Badger and John, then to Billy. He was hardly likely to go to the police, having been the one who did the deed. Why did he worry so? If the police can't find Gerald, then they should all be safe.

***

Helen Prescott wrestled with her conscious but had finally decided that she should volunteer her suspicions that Gerald had indeed purchased a narrowboat and was moving around the canals of England's waterways undetected.

Making up her mind, she picked up D.I. Harris's card and dialled his number. She waited a short time before a female voice announced that she was through to Detective Inspector Harris's office, and how could she help?

Helen gave her name. "I had a conversation with D.I. Harris, and he left me his card to call him if I thought of anything ease of importance. I felt that I might have an additional piece of information that he might like to check out."

"Please hold the line, and I'll check if the inspector is free to take the call."

Barely a minute had passed before he came on the line. "How nice to hear from you once again."

Helen relayed her information about a narrowboat called Restless Spirit and how she'd come to hear about it. D.I. Harris thanked her, and as he closed the call, he looked at his notes.

She was right. If he'd purchased a narrowboat, the crafty bugger would be gliding up and down the waterways unimpeded since there were no roadblocks on canals.

He rallied his force together and tasked them to find out if any county in the UK had a new record made with the Canal & River Trust for a narrowboat called Restless Spirit.

He then returned to his office smiling. He had a good

feeling about this lead. A very good feeling indeed.

***

The unsavoury character rang the police from a phone he liberated from a school kid.

He asked if they would pay him some of the money in advance if he gave them information on the gang.

The reply was non-committal.

"Check out this guy," he said anyway and gave them a name and address. "He's been doing a lot of night-time journeys lately. I'll call you again soon to see if you're going to pay me for my help."

He smashed the phone and dumped it in the bin. *Let them try and trace that,* he thought.

***

Robert woke the following morning to a bright-looking day. He stretched, rubbed his belly, and poured boiling water over his tea bag.

He wandered over to his bookings for the week and again gave thought to expanding his business. Robert had been passing occasional jobs of removal business to Adrian, AKA the Wall, since the France to Oxford shared job, and those jobs were now mounting up. Maybe it was time to venture into buying another removal van to enhance his business.

He got dressed after his breakfast and went downstairs just as the garage doors swung open.

Badger wasn't alone.

"These coppers were waiting outside the garage doors, guv. They want a private word with you."

Robert swallowed hard, then gathered himself together and advanced to the two law officers. He held out his hand in greeting, a smile on his face as if they were long lost friends.

They shook hands and showed their badges and warrant cards to Robert. "My name is Detective Loven, and this is PC Raith."

Behind them, doors were slamming as the men got the

removal vans sorted to go out on the allotted jobs.

"How can I help you, gentlemen?"

"Can we go somewhere a little quieter, please, sir?" asked Detective Loven, "I have a few questions that I think you might be able to answer."

Robert' stomach lurched, but he maintained his composure. "Let's go upstairs to my home. It'll be a little quieter there." He led the way, followed by the detective and the constable.

He closed the door behind them, and although noise could be heard, it didn't impinge on the conversation.

"Please take a seat, and if I can help you, I will happily do so," he said.

Detective Loven sat down in an easy chair, but the constable took one of the dining room chairs and sat on that. Robert noted this: it was to give the constable an easy path to stop him if he made a move they didn't like, like running for the door.

He was a sturdy guy and not someone Robert would like to upset. Robert sat in his easy chair opposite the detective. "So, how can I help you?"

Detective Loven leaned forward as if he were going to place something on the small table between them. "We have received information that you've been doing removals at night that are illegal."

Robert frowned. "Well, yes, we do removals at night, usually because the client wants the furniture to arrive the following morning. Has one of our customers complained to you rather than come to us?"

"No, sir," he said, making it sound as if it was saying cur. "This information implied that your removal business has extended to removing items from homes when the owners haven't secured your services."

"Theft! Who could suggest such a thing? I run a very tight and honest business here, and that also includes my limo hire business." Robert was on a roll now as the offended and innocently accused businessman. "I don't know who gave you this information, but I'll bet that it's one of my rivals. If this slander gets out, they'll get the advantage of my business going down the drain. Who told you this pack of lies? Do you have proof of this claim against me? I'd like to see it."

"I'm afraid I'm not at liberty to disclose that information, but we needed to substantiate their claim…or not, as the case may be."

"So, let me get this right. Someone has come into your police station and told you that I've been stealing property from homes while running my two businesses. They haven't given you any proof of this—it's just what they think. Is that about right, Detective Loven?"

"That is about it, sir," said Detective Loven as he wriggled uncomfortably, clearly realising how lame everything sounded.

"Right, then I think you should at least tell me who your informant is."

"As I said, sir," said Detective Loven, "I can't do that, but I think I have enough information having interviewed you—"

"Accused, you mean, detective," said Robert.

"As I was saying, sir, having talked to you, I think we can discount this unsubstantiated claim, and I'll be talking to my superior about our meeting and will be advising him to drop all interest on. this claim."

"Thank you, Detective Loven, but I wish you were at liberty to tell me who laid this at my door. However, I respect your confidentiality on this, and as long as my standing in this business isn't affected by any leaks from your end, I shall be happy."

Detective Loven and the constable shook hands with him. Robert escorted them down to the garage. All the vans were out of the garage, and the last one was parked outside ready to go.

Robert opened the wicket door and they stepped through onto the path outside.

As they walked down to their car, Robert gave the thumbs up to Badger, who grinned and started on his way to pick up someone's home, pack it into the van, and then move it all to wherever they wanted it to go.

Robert shut the door and went back upstairs, feeling a lot happier now that he'd fended off the first attack by the police. But who could the snake have been?

CHAPTER TWENTY-SEVEN

September / October

Two weeks passed before the break came for the police. A call came from Birmingham Canal Trust. The desk sergeant answered the call and when the caller announced he had information about a narrowboat named Restless Spirit, he asked the caller to hold while he patched him through to the inspector in charge.

Inspector Harris took the call. "Thank you for calling. I understand you have some information about a boat called Restless Spirit."

"Good morning, inspector. My name is Laurence Swift, and I deal with mooring and utility fees for the Birmingham Canal Trust. I received a red flag notice for this boat, but on checking, it wasn't someone who had moved without paying the fees; this was a police notice. A narrowboat had just moored up in the centre of Birmingham, and a fee for sewage disposal, electricity connection, and water top-up had been paid in the name of G Wickware. My people have made all of the connections requested and a sewage operation is due later today. What would you like us to do now?"

D.I. Harris replied, "Please do everything the owner asked, just as any other boat request would be responded to and leave it to them. Thank you for the info." He finished the call.

Moves could now be set in motion for an arrest on suspicion of robbery and being complicit to attempted murder. This would have to be co-ordinated by his colleagues in the Birmingham district. First, the arrest warrant.

The next day, early in the morning, Birmingham police officers boarded the boat and woke Gary Wickware, who they found still in his bed. The detective in charge said to a bleary-eyed scruffy person in front of him, "I have here an arrest warrant for a person named Gary Wickware. I have reason to believe that person is you. Can you confirm this, please?"

"Well, yes, but what's this all about?"

"I am arresting you, Gary Wickware, in connection with police investigations into a robbery and attempted murder. You do not have to say anything, but it may harm your defence if you do not mention, when questioned, something which you later rely on in court. Anything you do say may be taken and given as evidence. You will remain in jail while a prompt and effective investigation can be carried out, including an interview at the police station. The arrest is also necessary to prevent you taking action to leave the country."

They handcuffed Gary Wickware and escorted him to the local police station to await transport down to London to be interviewed by officers involved with the case. Local officers went through the canal boat, bagging up anything that could help with the investigation.

Two detectives arrived on the last day of September and accompanied the arrested man to a vehicle, he was then locked in the back of it, then driven down to London and on down to the **southeast division** police station for questioning.

They booked him in, took him to a cell, and with his handcuffs removed, locked him in it. Throughout, when asked a question, he refused to answer.

The man in the cell looked nothing like the smart person in the photo acting as Gerald Portman; he had a large beard and moustache, and with rather unkempt long hair, he looked more like a tramp. His fingerprints however spoke for him, confirming he was indeed Gary Wickware, AKA, Gerald Portman.

Now it was just the question and answering that must start very soon. He had asked for his solicitor, and he was due to attend the first questioning in a few days' time. Meanwhile, Gary Wickware, aka Gerald Portman, was given the chance to tidy himself up but he categorically refused.

***

Helen heard the news of the arrest by a phone call from a grateful D. I. Harris. He confirmed that he was a known criminal, but his name was not Gerald Portman.

It was later when she read the article in the newspaper, that she became more aware, that her ex-lover had well and truly used her. His interest in art, and also in her, was a side line to help with his lifestyle, and there had been no possibility for a marriage with him to her.

Robert read the article in dismay. Once Gerald started answering the inevitable questions, Robert could expect a visit from the police. He called Badger and arranged a quick meeting at his home to lay out a plan.

***

D.I. Wainwright and Constable Sandra Villiers read the message they had received from D.I. Harris.

The arrest of Gary Wickware was pleasing but he wished it had been his team who had arrested him.

They were gathering evidence and were going to start the interview with a solicitor present tomorrow.

***

Gill and Sheila received a phone call from D.I. Wainwright, who informed them that the arrest of their dance host had been made, and he hoped to get more news about the gang in the near future.

***

At ten o'clock, after an hour with his solicitor, Gary Wickware was taken into the interview room.

D.I. Harris said, "For the sake of the recording, in this room are D.I. Harris, Detective Alan Tarton, and Gary Wickware, aka Gerald Portman, and his solicitor, Mr Stanley Arscott."

"I must ask you, inspector," said Mr Arscott, "to not refer to my client as Gerald Portman in any form. You have no evidence that he was ever on a cruise ship, that he had anything to do with an attempted murder, or even that he has taken on that alias at all."

"The charges will stand for now. That's why we're having this interview, under caution. Does your client understand this?"

Mr Arscott spoke quietly to his client, then said, "Please explain the term 'under caution.'"

"It means that the evidence we have obtained so far suggests that you may have committed an offence. This interview gives you the opportunity to provide an explanation of the events. However, if we find any evidence during the interview that you have committed an offence, you may be prosecuted."

Mr Arscott consulted quietly with his client once again. "My client will answer any questions he can."

D.I. Harris leaned forward. "I would like to start with your impersonation of a dead man by assuming his name and working on cruise ships. Do you admit that you were on several cruise ships working under the name of Gerald Portman?"

"No."

"Are you denying that you worked on cruise ships using a false passport and identity?"

"Yes."

"I would like to show you some pass cards taken from the cruise ships with a picture of you on all of them. Please look at the screen at the end of the table."

A photo came up of a card with Gerald Portman and a photo of a clean-shaven smart man.

"Looks nothing like me."

Another from a different ship came up, and again, received the same response.

"Can you tell me how you got out to the Caribbean when there is no record of your exit from England, but there is for Gerald Portman."

"No comment."

"Mr Wickware, you can continue to refuse to answer these questions, but if you don't cooperate, you could find yourself with even deeper problems. Drug smuggling comes to mind. We have evidence of your return to the UK, the flight times, a video of you in the airport, and you checking in for the return flight. If you continue to deny you assumed a dead man's name, we will need to examine how you could get to the Caribbean illegally, and what possible purpose you could have to do that."

He looked at his solicitor, who whispered something to him. "Yes, I did work on the cruise ships," Wickware said. "I got a passport with a new name, since they wouldn't employ me because of my police record. I'm a good dancer, and it paid well."

"So, it's now on record that you left England on a Saga cruise ship using a false passport and returned using your own. Is that correct?"

"Yes."

"And you have worked a several different cruise ships as a dance host?"

"Yes."

"Tell me, Mr Wickware, why did you leave the last ship and fly home?"

"I was fed up with dancing and listening to their inane conversations."

"This suddenly came over you did it?"

"Yes."

"The fact that you got a message from an associate in England, informing you that a woman had been killed, had no bearing on your decision I assume."

"Don't reply to that," interjected Mr Arscott. "Inspector, you have no proof that my client had anything to do with any attempted murder. Indeed, you admit he was in the Caribbean at the time of the event, so how could he be involved? You will need to supply proof to me and my client that he had some form of involvement, otherwise, all you have is his admitting he obtained a job with a false passport."

D.I. Harris stood and said, "This interview is now terminated pending further investigation. Your client will be returned to his cell pending a criminal charge of impersonating another man by procuring a false passport. We will interview him about this and advise you when we're going to do so."

Gary Wickware was taken back to his cell and his legal

aid was left knowing that a lesser charge, once made, would cause his client's release pending a trial.

The police needed to establish the link from the cruise ship to the robbery that they thought he masterminded.

***

The unsavoury character had rung the police from another phone liberated from a youth who had walked past him as he waited for a target.

He again rang the police. "Are you going to pay me some of the money in advance for the information he gave you on the gang that was working at night nicking peoples stuff."

After waiting and giving his name, he was told, "I'm sorry, the information was useless. We have no proof."

He closed the call and scrapped the phone. *Proof, eh? I'll give them proof.*

Now he was waiting for another target, someone he'd overheard talking about doing business on burglar alarms for his mate John Brooks.

Billy didn't notice Alan Harding waiting for him, but when Harding's fist landed into his stomach taking the wind from him, he was soon acutely aware.

Harding pulled him up and slapped his face hard. "Now, Billy boy, you're going to tell me all about your night-time adventures with John Brooks and the rest of them. Then you're going to come with me for a little walk. If you don't want me to start cutting you, do as I say. And speak clearly. I don't want any snivelling."

Billy tried to get free from the hold but another blow to his stomach and a kick to his back while he was on the floor gave him little choice.

"If I tell you anything, they'll find you and beat you up. Just let me go, Alan, and forget it."

Alan pulled out the phone from Billy's pocket and took a photo of Billy. "That's a photo of you now. The next one will be you in a pool of blood. Now, talk to me, Billy," he said with a reminder kick to Billy's thigh.

"What do you want to know? Did your brother Troy send

you?"

"I ask the questions, Tell me about the visits at night to rob people."

"Oh, Alan, not that. They'll sort us both out if I tell you anything about that."

Another kick. "Talk to me, Billy."

Predictably, Billy caved and told Alan all about their perfect thefts.

"And was Priceright in on it too, or doesn't he know about Badger, John, and you?"

"He's the gaffer."

"Thank you, Billy. Now you can get up, so we can go for a nice walk."

"Where are you taking me, Alan?"

"Nowhere far, old son. We're going to have a chat with a friend of mine."

Billy was now very scared, but with Alan being a much bigger and stronger bloke, he had very little choice, and with another punch into his stomach, Billy went with Alan, hopeful for the best.

It was a painful thirty minutes of occasional punches and kicks before they arrived at the police station.

Alan pushed Billy up to the desk. "This is Billy Drayton. I've brought him to you because he's part of the gang that you're looking for who robbed that old bird and nearly killed her. Now, can I have my reward money?"

"Tell me, sir, how do you know he's one of them?"

Alan took out the mobile phone and placed it on the desk. "His confession is on there."

"From the looks of him, you beat him up to get it."

"Check it out, get the rest in, and they'll soon start squealing. You've got them bang to rights, so when do I get my money?"

"I shall need your name and address and a phone number to contact you once we've checked the information you have provided is correct."

Alan said, "I gave you all this before. My name is Alan Harding, and I gave your lot the information, so I claim the reward."

The duty sergeant then asked, "And who owns this phone with the information on it?"

"Billy does. I used the one in his pocket."

The duty sergeant phoned for someone to come down and a detective arrived within a few minutes. He went over what had been said and listened to the recording that had been made. They then took Billy through to the interview room, leaving Alan at the desk.

"I'll expect my reward soon, now you got yer gang," he said and left.

*** *

Robert was roused from a deep sleep by the ringing of his doorbell. After pulling on his dressing gown, he walked downstairs to the wicket gate and unlocked the door.

"Good morning, Mr Price. So sorry to wake you at this unearthly time, but we would like you to help us with our enquiries, and it can't wait until the morning."

Robert looked at the same two officers who had visited just a short time ago. He stepped back, and said, "You'd better come in then."

Both stepped through the doorway and followed Robert upstairs to his home.

They again introduced themselves, showing their badges and warrant cards to Robert. My name is Detective Loven and this is PC Raith."

"Would you be good enough to get dressed, sir?" Detective Loven asked. "You'll be helping us by answering questions at the police station."

"Am I to assume you are arresting me for something, detective?"

"Not at this precise moment, sir, but if you refuse to help us by coming with us voluntarily, then I will be forced to arrest you. The end result will be just the same."

"Very well. I'll go and get dressed."

As he went to go, Detective Loven said, "My constable will go with you, just in case you fall out of the window. We wouldn't want you to do that, would we?" he said with an alligator grin on his face.

Robert looked at the towering block of human that came towards him, turned, and went to his bedroom.

The human block stood at the door as Robert got dressed.

"Right then, detective, I'm willing to accompany you to your police station to help in any way I can. Do I need a solicitor?"

"That will depend on your answers, sir, but for now, no. Remember that we're not arresting you—yet."

Robert locked the door and got into the police car, with the block sitting next to him in the back seat. When they got to the police station, Robert was taken into an interview room, where he was asked to sit, and then Detective Loven and another police officer sat in chairs opposite him.

"We're going to tape this interview, and so I'll be asking you some questions I've asked you before. You don't have to answer them, and you can ask for a solicitor at any time."

Robert sat visibly shaken, his face had paled, and his hands were shaking. He looked across at Robert and then went on, "You're not under arrest, and you don't have to consent to being interviewed, though this could work against you in the event of further investigation."

He placed a glossy piece of paper in front of him and the constable lifted a thin file from the side of him and placed it on the table. "I am Detective Brian Wright, and my assistant officer is Constable David Greeves. Also, in this room is— could you say your name, please?"

Robert leaned forward. "Robert Price, also known by my friends as Priceright."

"Thank you, Mr Price. I have previously asked you questions about a suspected offence, and now new information has come to light. Mr Price, this a photo of a man in custody, the photo is marked as A." The detective turned the glossy paper over and pushed it to Robert. "Do you know this man, Mr. Price?"

Robert picked it up and looked at a photo of a battered Billy. "Yes, I do. Is he in hospital or something?"

"No, Mr Price. He's in one of our custody cells."

"I hope this didn't happen while he was in police custody.

Whatever has he done to deserve this?"

Both officers looked at each other, then to Robert.

"Mr. Price," said the detective, "we don't beat confessions out of people. We simply ask the questions, as we are here with you."

"I'm glad to hear it. So what's he done, and who did this to him?"

"He has given us a tape recording where he confessed to helping you rob homes at night, including the one that went wrong on the southwest coast."

"Billy has helped with our removal business, filling in when someone is out ill, on holiday, or when they've had other appointments." Robert lifted his hands and opened them on the table palms up, knowing that this was a sign of openness from a book he had read. "As far as I know, he's never been with us on any of our overnight runs, but I can check and show you the books."

"So, you're saying that he has only worked for your legitimate business and nothing else?"

"Well, I wouldn't consider him for the limo business. I prefer an older person for that. They tend to be steadier drivers."

"Are you sure that this is the truth? Remember, he volunteered this information to us."

"Was he beaten half to death by one of your people, or did he make the tape before he beat himself up? Come on, detective, you're wasting my time with your fishing expedition. I've told you that I know Billy, but I didn't bash him around, and if you didn't, then who did? Could it be that someone did this to him, then planted a tape on him to direct you away from your actual investigation?"

"Very well, Mr. Price. This interview is terminated at," he checked his watch, "4:37 a.m."

"You should get that lad looked at. He's clearly in a bad way."

"The doctor is with him now, sir, and we won't be charging him for anything at the moment. We will take you home now and thank you. Oh, do you own a passport, sir? Only as this is an ongoing case, we wouldn't want you to take a holiday just yet."

CHAPTER TWENTY-EIGHT

October

Robert sat in his favourite chair feeling that this time he wasn't going to win.

Making his mind up about something he had given thought to for a while now, he went down to the limos and drove one out of the garage. It was quite a journey that he made but thanks to the police interview, it was still early and there was very little traffic on the road.

Almost three hours later, he arrived, did what he wanted to do, and set about driving back to his home. Once he had put the limo back and saw that the removal vans were out and on their way, he searched for a box and set about packing it for a parcel delivery.

He wrote one word on a small card and then put it inside of the box. Once everything was sealed, he headed out into the early morning drizzle, pulling his collar up around his neck. He caught a taxi, gave the address, and then sat back to wait.

On arrival at his destination, he asked the taxi driver to wait and went into Adrian's office.

"Bloody hell, you look like you've seen a ghost. What's up?"

Robert said he had a parcel that he wanted to send, but he wanted to delay it. He explained that he only wanted it if he was arrested.

Adrian frowned. "It's not drugs, is it?"

"No, you daft sod. What would I want with drugs? It's something that doesn't belong to me, but it was removed by someone I know. I want to return it so that person will feel a little happier." Robert placed a fifty-pound note on the top. "That will cover the cost of a recorded delivery."

"Okay, Robert, you and I have always had a good working relationship, and it sounds as if you're going to take the fall for someone, so yes, I'll do this for you."

"That's all I can ask. Thanks, Adrian," he said and they shook hands.

Once home, Robert sat in his favourite chair, feeling that a weight on his shoulders had been lifted. He wriggled to get a more comfortable position, and in a few moments, fell into a restful and deep sleep.

***

D.I. Harris rang D.I. Wainwright and put a question to him. Both had been keeping the other up to date with events but they kept coming up against buffers. On each occasion, they had failed to link any of the suspects together, and there was only one piece to the jigsaw that could do that.

D.I. Harris asked, "Is there was any possibility that Mrs Chancel could come up to the southeast division headquarters to help with the investigation? If your superintendent could allow you to accompany her, I would also like to meet you."

Having given the request much thought, the superintendent said, "If Mrs Chancel is willing to go, then I think you should go." He also said, "If Mrs Blakeney wished to accompany Mrs Chancel, she should also go. She might also be able to help in some way to try a full attack on the suspects."

***

The doorbell rang, and Sheila answered it, opening the door to see D.I. Wainwright standing under the covered porch with a bunch of flowers in his hand. Behind his bulk, the figure of Sandra hunched up in the rain and wind caused her to smile.

Typical bloke. He's dry; never mind his help.

"May we come in? We're both getting rather wet out here."

Well, one of you is. She stepped back and allowed them into the hall.

"Let me take your coats, then go on in and sit down."

D.I. Wainwright gave her the flowers with no words, then once they had hung their coats, they went into the lounge.

"Nice to see you back in your own home now." He looked

around. "You look so much better now than when I last saw you here."

"Well, that wouldn't be hard, would it? I was nearly dead the last time you saw me here! Is that what's brought you out in the rain to see me?"

All her marbles are still intact. "As we're not in my office, I'm here to ask you for some help, I think I'll pick up on your offer of use of first names once again. So here goes, Sheila. You remember you said that there was one thing for sure, you would never forget the face of your attacker? Do you still feel that way?"

"Yes, I would most certainly know him if he was in front of me."

"How would you like to try to pick him out of an identity parade?"

"Could Gill come with me? She didn't see him, of course, but I'd love her there for moral support?"

"Yes, of course. That would be no problem at all. We'll collect you, stay with you, and bring you back. I can assure you that neither of you will be in any danger."

"Any time you wish then—oh, you didn't say what your name was, did you?"

He smiled. "No, I didn't, did I?"

***

Gary Wickware and Billy Thomas were brought to the Central southeast division, with Billy looking much better. Robert Price was asked to attend and when he refused, they arrested him. They also asked if all of Robert's employees could present themselves at the station, and they were brought down under caution.

When the car arrived, Sheila and Gill were escorted to the office of D. I. Harris. He shook hands with them both. "Mrs Chancel, we need you to identify for us a person you might know. We would like you also Mrs Blakeney to do the same."

As both agreed, he turned to Sheila and said, "Mrs Chancey, you have said you would recognise your attacker if you saw him again. I would like you to see if you can pick out the person you feel was your attacker in an identity parade. If you are happy to do this, I can get the second interview room readied."

Ten minutes later, one at a time, they were ushered into a room that looked into the interview room and then asked, "Do you recognised this man, and if so, what name did you know him as,"

Both had confirmed that this was Gerald Portman, their dance host.

Next, they were taken to a large room and then told to wait while they got a line of people ready for an identity parade. Once it was ready, Sheila was asked to look at each person, and if she recognised anyone, she should say the number and point to them.

She asked if Gill could be in the room with her and walked with the policewoman beside her. "Yes, but she can't walk with you, only the officer can. I'm sorry."

Sheila looked at Gill who nodded slightly, then said, "You can do this, Sheila, you really can. Sheila entered the room with the policewoman by her side, and Gill stood with her back to the wall watching as they walked slowly down the line. Sheila stopped at each person looking at each face for a few moments. She came to number seven and stopped abruptly. She'd recognise that boy's face until the day she really did die. She pointed at him. "How could you? You nearly killed me!" She broke into tears, and Gill rushed to her, wrapped her arm around Sheila's shoulders, and said softly, "It's okay Sheila, you did it, now it's up to the police. Offering her a tissue she added, "He can't hurt you now,"

As the policeman began to guide her away, she heard a voice say, "I'm sorry, missus, I didn't mean to. You frightened me out of my skin when you sat up like that."

Sheila was ushered out just as an officer began to say the words she had heard so often on TV programmes: "You do not have to say anything. However, it may harm your defence if you do not mention when questioned something that you later rely on in court."

The door closed as she sobbed and hung onto Gill. They

followed the constable back through to where the two inspectors waited.

"Well done, Sheila. A nice cup of tea, I think. Let's set you down in a chair, and you rest for a moment. D.I. Harris has some more questions to ask, and I think we'll then be able to say, with my granny sleuths' help, we have busted a major gang of crooks."

***

Robert waited in another room, a feeling of dread coming over him.

The door opened, and two officers came in and sat opposite Robert and his solicitor. They went through the rules about recording the interview and once that was done, the inspector placed a photo of Gerald in front of him and said, "We have arrested Billy Drayton, a confessed member of your gang. We're processing all your employees, and we'll soon have all of your gang. We know that Billy Drayton hit Mrs Chancel when he was rifling through things in her bedroom. Once we have our list of the drivers who went on these raids, we'll then charge you all. If you choose to help now, that will go in your favour."

Robert spoke quietly to his solicitor for a moment then said, "You can let all the other drivers go. They had nothing to do with it. I've spoken to my two helpers, and they both agreed that I should make it easy for them and me by naming themselves."

The two officers looked at each other, and then one said, "And they are?"

"Tell them that I have confessed and that I asked you to ask them to tell you themselves."

They closed the interview and Robert slouched forward as the door closed.

***

Both Barry and his son John confessed to their part in the robbery, but both denied any part in hurting Sheila.

Both were interviewed with Robert's solicitor in attendance and when asked if they knew this man when they showed a photo of Gary Wickware, they both said they knew him as the partner in the robbery venture.

***

The officers returned to Robert's interview room and placed the photo of Gary Wickware in front of him. "Do you recognise this man?"

"Yes, he introduced himself to me as Gerald Masters, but I found out that he was really Gerald Portman. He was my partner and the one who masterminded all of this."

"Would it surprise you that Gerald Masters isn't his real name either? His real name is Gary Wickware."

"Nothing could surprise me about that man."

They got the custody officer and went through the process of booking each and every one of the offenders, then announced that the others could leave.

Before they went, Robert asked if they could tell the other drivers to go and see Adrian Waldron who would most likely offer them a job, given that Robert wouldn't be running his businesses for some time.

***

It was eight days since they had returned from their journey to the southeast division police centre.

Gill, D.I Harris, and Sheila were sat in her house, a bunch of flowers in a vase looking superb on the table, a gift from the inspector.

"You know, I am still curious, why was it that you never told me your first name."

"Yes, well, I didn't want my colleagues in the office to know, but if it stays in the confines of this house, then it's Claude."

"Yes, I can see why you wouldn't want anyone to know that," said Gill.

The inspector left a few moments later, again thanking the

ladies for all of their help.

A few moments later, the doorbell rang, and Sheila answered it to find a parcel delivery that had to be signed for.

She couldn't remember ordering anything and wondered if it might be a thank you gift from the police at the southeast division. They had a lot to thank her and Gill for, after all.

She signed for the heavy box and took it into the kitchen to get scissors. When she opened it, she began to cry.

Gill came over to her, but seeing what was in the box, just stood near her.

Sheila she pulled first one and then the second statue from the box.

She had her memory back with her once again. She rubbed her husband's statue tenderly and read the single word on a piece of paper.

Sorry.

What's Your Story?

Global Wordsmiths, CIC, provides an all-encompassing service for all writers, ranging from basic proofreading and cover design to development editing, typesetting, and eBook services. A major part of our work is charity and community focused, delivering writing projects to under-served and under-represented groups across Nottinghamshire, giving voice to the voiceless and visibility to the unseen.

To learn more about what we offer, visit: www.globalwords.co.uk

A selection of books by Global Words Press:
Desire, Love, Identity: with the National Justice Museum
Aventuras en México: Farmilo Primary School
Life's Whispers: Journeys to the Hospice
Times Past: with The Workhouse, National Trust
World At War: Farmilo Primary School
Young at Heart with AGE UK
In Different Shoes: Stories of Trans Lives
Patriotic Voices: Stories of Service

Self-published authors working with Global Wordsmiths:
Steve Bailey
Ravenna Castle
Jackie D
CJ DeBarra
Dee Griffiths
Iona Kane
Ray Martin
Emma Nichols
Dani Lovelady Ryan
Erin Zak

Printed in Great Britain
by Amazon